W9-AMU-724

Her emotions were clearly written on her features

Simon hardened his heart against the anxiety and confusion he saw there. She said, "I shouldn't have talked so much.... I'll be in Jim's room. You'll call if you need anything?"

He nodded, making no move to touch her or kiss her good-night. She made the smallest gesture toward him, then withdrew her hand, her face full of bewilderment. Simon lay back on the pillows and closed his eyes, and heard her leave the room. A few moments later the light went out in the living room and the springs creaked in Jim's bedroom.

He felt as though something inexpressibly wonderful had been held out to him; but just as he was about to take it, it had been snatched away.

He wanted Shea. But he couldn't have her.

Although born in England, *SANDRA FIELD* has lived most of her life in Canada; she says the silence and emptiness of the north speaks to her particularly. While she enjoys traveling, and passing on her sense of a new place, she often chooses to write about the city that is now her home. Sandra says, "I write out of any experience. I have learned that love with its joys and its pains is all-important. I hope this knowledge enriches my writing, and touches a chord in you, the reader."

Books by Sandra Field

HARLEQUIN PRESENTS
1336—LOVE AT FIRST SIGHT
1416—THE LAND OF MAYBE
1448—HAPPY ENDING
1506—SAFETY IN NUMBERS
1557—TAKEN BY STORM
1598—ONE-NIGHT STAND
1646—TRAVELLING LIGHT

HARLEQUIN ROMANCE
2480—SIGHT OF A STRANGER
2577—THE TIDES OF SUMMER

writing as Jan MacLean
2348—WHITE FIRE
2537—ALL OUR TOMORROWS

writing as Jocelyn Haley
DREAM OF DARKNESS

Don't miss any of our special offers. Write to us at the following address for information on our newest releases.

Harlequin Reader Service
U.S.: 3010 Walden Ave., P.O. Box 1325, Buffalo, NY 14269
Canadian: P.O. Box 609, Fort Erie, Ont. L2A 5X3

SANDRA FIELD

Wildfire

Harlequin Books

TORONTO • NEW YORK • LONDON
AMSTERDAM • PARIS • SYDNEY • HAMBURG
STOCKHOLM • ATHENS • TOKYO • MILAN
MADRID • WARSAW • BUDAPEST • AUCKLAND

ISBN 0-373-11709-4

WILDFIRE

Copyright © 1994 by Sandra Field.

This edition published by arrangement with Harlequin Enterprises B.V.

® and TM are trademarks of the publisher. Trademarks indicated with
® are registered in the United States Patent and Trademark Office, the
Canadian Trade Marks Office and in other countries.

Printed in U.S.A.

CHAPTER ONE

HE WAS in love.

Smiling to himself, Simon Greywood rested his paddle across the gunwales, the canoe sliding silently through the mirror-smooth water. It was early enough in the morning that mist, cool and intangible, was still rising from the lake, wreathing the reeds and granite boulders that edged the shore in phantasmagorical folds. Although birds were singing in the forest, some of them so sweetly that they made his throat ache, their cries merely scratched the surface of a silence so absolute as to be a force in itself.

The silence of wilderness, he thought. A wilderness as different from the city he had left only two weeks ago as could be imagined. In London, no matter what the hour of day or night, there was always the underlying snarl of traffic, the sense of people pressing in on all sides...whereas here, on a lake deep in the Nova Scotian forest, there was not another human being in sight. He loved it here. Felt almost as though in some strange way he had come home.

From the corner of his eye he caught movement. A wet brown head was swimming purposefully toward him, churning a V-shaped wake in the water. Wondering if it could be a beaver, for Jim had told him there was a dam in the stillwater near the head of the lake, Simon sat motionless. Within fifteen feet of the canoe the animal suddenly veered away from him, slapped its tail on the lake with a crack like a gunshot, and in a flurry of spray dived beneath the water.

The tail had been broad and flat, highly effective as a warning signal. So it was a beaver. Chuckling softly, Simon picked up his paddle again and stroked through the channel between the two lakes, carefully avoiding a couple of rocks that lay just below the surface. The water level was down, Jim had told him, because it had been such a hot, dry summer.

He had not paddled as far as this second lake before. What had Jim called it? Maynard's Lake? Not a name that in any way expressed the serene beauty of the still, dark water that reflected in perfect symmetry the rocks and trees surrounding the lake and the small white clouds that hung above it.

Following the shore, he worked on the Indian stroke that Jim had been teaching him, a stroke that enabled him to stay on course without ever lifting the paddle out of the water and thus to move as silently as was possible. Best way to come across wildlife, Jim had assured him, describing how he had once got within forty feet of a moose by using that particular stroke.

The shoreline meandered down the lake in a series of coves, each lush with ferns and the pink blooms of bog laurel. The mist was slowly dissipating as the sun gained warmth. All the tensions that had driven Simon for as many years as he could remember seemed to be seeping away under the morning's spell; he felt utterly at peace in a way that was new to him. And he had Jim to thank for it. Jim, his brother, from whom he had been separated for nearly twenty-five years...

A series of loud splashes came from the next cove, shattering the quiet and his own reflective mood; it was as though some large animal had entered the water and was wading through it. A moose? A bear? In spite of himself, Simon felt a shiver of atavistic fear ripple along his nerves. He might feel as though he was at home here. But in terms of actual experience of the wilderness he was a raw beginner. He'd do well to remember that.

He edged nearer the granite boulders that hid him from view of the next cove. There was a gap between the rocks, too narrow for his canoe, but wide enough that he should be able to see what was causing the disturbance without himself being seen. Sculling gently, he came parallel with the gap, and as he did so the splashing ceased with dramatic suddenness.

He had not dreamed it, though. The surface of the water in the cove was stirred into ripples and tiny wavelets, on which the lily pads placidly bobbed. But of the perpetrator of the ripples there was no sign.

Moose, he was almost sure, did not dive. Did bears? He had no idea. Holding himself ready to do a swift back-up stroke if the situation called for it, Simon waited to see what creature would emerge from the lake. Another beaver? A loon?

A head broke the surface, swimming away from him. Long hair streamed from the skull back into the water as, in a smooth, sinuous curve of naked flesh, the woman dived beneath the lake again. Tiny air bubbles rose to the top, and the ripples spread slowly outward.

Simon took a deep breath, wondering if he was indeed dreaming. He had been under the impression that Jim's cabin was the last little outpost of civilization on this chain of lakes; certainly his brother had not mentioned that anyone else lived farther out than he. So who was this woman, who had appeared and disappeared like some spirit of the lake?

As if in answer to his question, she burst up out of the water again, her profile to him this time, the sun glinting on her wet cheeks and white teeth, for she was smiling in sheer pleasure. The force of her stroke brought, momentarily, the gleam of her shoulders and the smooth swell of her breasts into sight, inexpressibly beautiful. Then, in a flash of bare thighs, she knifed below the water.

His nails digging into the polished shaft of his paddle, Simon waited for her to reappear. When she did, she was facing him. But the rising sun was full in her face, and he was sure he was invisible to her.

He knew two things with an immediacy that knocked him off balance.

First, of course, he knew he did not want to disturb her in her play; for play it was, as innocent and joyful as that of a young otter. To frighten her, or alert her to his presence, was the last thing he wanted.

He could not tell what color her eyes were, nor her hair, clinging as it was to her head. Nor, even with his artist's trained eye, could he discern details of her face: she was too far away, and the sun shone too brightly on her features. What he received was an impression of both motion and emotion, of vivid life intensely embodied. She was a creature of the moment, this woman. Most certainly she was no lake spirit. That was too ethereal a designation by far. She was a woman of flesh and blood who was, he would be willing to bet, as much in love with life as he himself was in love with the wilderness.

As she rolled over onto her back with easy grace and began splashing away from him, her breasts hidden in the spray and then exposed to the sun, their pink tips shining wetly, he admitted to himself what the second thing was. He desired her. Instantly and unequivocally, as he had not desired a woman for a long time. If he were to obey his instincts he would drive the canoe around the rocks, scoop her up and then make love to her with a passion he'd thought he had lost.

Sure, Simon, a voice jeered in his ear. Canoes aren't designed for lovemaking. Both of you would end up in the lake. Anyway, a woman as vital as that one might want to choose her partner herself. Assuming she hasn't already got one. Get real, as Jim would say.

The woman rolled over onto her stomach, her spine a long, entrancing curve. But her mood had changed from play to work. For nearly fifteen minutes she swam back and forth parallel to the shore with a businesslike crawl, all her movements supple and strong. Then, diving again, she headed toward the shore.

Simon had sat as still as a statue for the entire fifteen minutes. He now brought the canoe around so as not to lose sight of her. Part of him was ashamed that he should watch her like any Peeping Tom; particularly when in such a setting she could not possibly be expecting anyone within miles of her. Intuitively he was sure she would not have played so artlessly in the water had she suspected human eyes were on her. But he could not help himself. Formidable as his willpower could be, and he knew just how formidable better than any other human being, it was not strong enough to make him drag his eyes away from her.

His mouth dry, he watched her get to her feet, the water waist-deep, waves caressing her hips. Her hair reached halfway down her back. Tossing her head, she flicked it back, before wading to the small sand beach at the farthest point of the cove.

She moved beautifully, with an unselfconscious grace that brought a lump to his throat. When she reached the sand, she stooped to pick up a bright red towel that was lying there. But instead of walking toward the trees she turned briefly to face the lake, the towel hanging from one hand like an ancient banner of war. Throwing back her head, she gave a delicious peal of laughter, in which was all her joy in the freshness of morning and the pleasure of her solitary swim.

The sound struck Simon to the heart, for in it was a quality that he had ground to dust in his own soul during the last ten years. He felt involuntary tears prick at the back of his eyes, and furiously willed them back. The woman had wrapped the towel around her body and was loping up the sand toward a venerable pine tree that overhung the beach. For the first time he saw, tucked among the tree trunks, a weathered cabin with a wide veranda and a stone chimney. Even as he watched, she disappeared among the trees in a flutter of scarlet. A few moments later he heard a screen door bang shut.

Simon let out his breath in a long sigh. His emotions were in chaos, a chaos he had no wish to analyze. He needed to get out of here. He needed to go back to Jim's cabin, to the world that was sane and normal and known. As he picked up his paddle, he briefly looked down into the water to check for rocks, and saw in its mirror his own face. It looked no different from the way it usually did; somehow he would have expected the last few minutes to have marked it in some way.

His hair was thick and unruly, blacker than the surface of the lake, while his eyes, in startling contrast, were as blue as a summer sky. His willpower, which had driven him for so many years, was matched by the hard line of his jaw and the uncompromising jut of his nose, features that gave his face character rather than conventional good looks. That he was attractive to women he

had long known and never really understood. His eye
for detail failed him when it came to his own counte-
nance: he was blind to the hint of sensuality in his mouth,
to all the shadings of emotion that his eyes could express, to the thickness of his dark lashes which con-
trasted so intriguingly with the strength in his cheekbones.

He might not understand why women gravitated to
him. He did know that there had never been a woman
he had chosen to pursue who had not gone willingly to
his bed. Willingly and soon. This he had come to take
for granted. What it had meant was that he had slept
with very few women in the last number of years, because what was easy and available was not always what
was desired.

Scowling down at his face, Simon plunged the paddle
into the water so that the reflection disappeared in a swirl
of ripples. He brought the canoe around with a couple
of strong sweeps, then began stroking back down the
lake as though all the demons of the underworld were
after him, digging his blade into the water so hard that
his wake was marked by miniature black whirlpools.

He had been in danger of being sucked into such a
whirlpool, he thought savagely, navigating the channel
into the next lake with less than his usual caution. So
he had seen a naked woman swimming in a lake. So
what? He had seen naked women before. Seen them,
painted them, made love to some of them. There was
no reason for him suddenly to be feeling as though he
was the only man in a world newly created, and she the
one woman fashioned for his delight. No reason for him
to feel as though all the warmth of the sun had fallen
into his lap, like a gift of the gods. No reason at all. He

was thirty-five years old, experienced and wise in the ways of the world. He was not sixteen.

As though mocking him, his inner eye presented him with a graphic image of the woman's sensuous play in the water, of her pleasure-drenched smile and her water-streaked breasts. It was an image that made nonsense of reason in a way that both infuriated and frightened him. Apart from anything else, he had no idea who she was. Perhaps she was a visitor who would be gone from here by the weekend. Perhaps she was happily married. Perhaps he would never see her again. And even if he did, would he recognize her?

Only if she's naked, the little voice sneered in his ear.

Go away, he growled. This is ridiculous! It makes no difference whether she's from Vancouver with a husband and ten children or from Halifax with a live-in boyfriend. He, Simon, had not come to Canada to get involved with a woman. He had come to get acquainted with his brother; and to break away from a city that had been stifling him. This unknown woman was nothing to him. Nothing!

Driven by his own thoughts, and despite the headwind that had sprung up, Simon made it back to Jim's cabin in record time. Physical action, as always, had made him feel better. Grinning ruefully to himself as he felt the twinges in his shoulder muscles, he tied the canoe to the dock. Then he strode up the path to the deck, took the steps in two quick leaps, and pulled open the screen door. It slammed shut behind him with a sound that struck into his memory: just so had another door on another cabin slammed shut half an hour ago.

Determined not to allow that aberrant turmoil of emotion to seize him again, equally determined not to ask a single question about the woman who lived in the cabin on Maynard's Lake, he said, "Mmm...smells good."

Jim was frying bacon in a cast-iron pan on the gas stove; his cabin, for all its rustic air, had all the modern conveniences. Turning over a rasher with a fork, he said casually, "You must have gone quite a way...see anything interesting?"

Jim was all that Simon was not, and in a group of people they would never have been taken for brothers. Ten years younger, four inches shorter, tow-haired where Simon had black hair, Jim had a sunny smile and an open nature, as far from the man of secrets that was his elder brother as a man could be. Jim was like a tabby cat stretched out in a patch of sunlight on the floor, purring in contentment; whereas Simon was like a wildcat, wary, deep-hidden in the shadows of the forest.

"I went as far as Maynard's Lake," Simon replied. "Shall I put some toast on?"

"Sure...how's your J-stroke doing?"

Simon grinned. "I'll have you know that I can actually canoe in a straight line, brother dear." He cut four slices of the thick molasses bread that was sold at the nearest bakery. "I might marry the woman who makes this bread," he added.

"You can't," Jim said amiably. "She's married to the local police chief who also happens to be the county's champion arm wrestler. Pass me the eggs, would you?"

As Simon took the carton of farm eggs out of the refrigerator and handed them to his brother, he said awkwardly, "You're a good teacher, Jim. Two weeks ago I'd never even been in a canoe. You've spent a lot of time with me—thanks."

Jim shot him a keen glance. But all he said was, "You're welcome. Can't have you going back to England never having experienced something as quintessentially Canadian as canoeing.''

''I even saw a beaver this morning. Plus several hundred maple trees.''

''Then you're practically a native.'' Jim laughed. Cracking a couple of eggs into the pan, he added, ''As I recall, the best canoe lesson we had was the one on rescue techniques—that was the morning you turned into a human being.''

After a tiny hesitation Simon said evenly, ''You believe in direct speech, don't you?''

''I say it like it is, yeah . . . life's too short for anything else. The first three or four days you were here I figured it was going to be one hell of a long summer.''

Simon remembered the lesson on rescue all too well. It had involved him standing upright in one canoe pulling Jim's swamped canoe up over the gunwales, and later hauling his brother out of the water, too. Jim had been pretending to be panic-stricken; it had been an interesting few minutes. Certainly it had been the day when the first of the barriers between the two men had fallen to the ground; Jim's memory was entirely accurate. ''Do you still feel that way? About the long summer, I mean.''

''No. Although, like an iceberg, nine-tenths of you stays beneath the surface.''

''That's the way I live,'' Simon said, exasperated.

Expertly Jim flipped the eggs over. ''That the reason it took you the best part of six weeks to answer my letter?''

Simon very carefully buttered the toast, taking his time. He said finally, ''When I first got here, I mentioned that things hadn't been going well for me lately. I'm in a rut as far as my painting's concerned, London feels like a prison—dammit, I don't even want to talk about it!''

He paused, knowing he had been guilty of understatement. For the past six months he had quite literally found himself unable to paint. In the north light of his studio he had spent hours standing in front of a blank canvas, paralyzed by its whiteness, its emptiness, its mute quality of waiting. Since the age of sixteen he had lived to paint. To find himself cut off from his life's blood had terrified him. And the more terrified he had become, the less able he had been even to hold a brush, let alone use it.

He took a ragged breath, knowing he had to pick up the thread of his story. ''When your letter came in April, it took me totally by surprise. I'd tried to trace you once, years ago, but the records had been destroyed in a fire, and that was that. There was nothing more I could do. So when I heard from you it was like a voice from the past. I wasn't even sure I wanted to look at that past. Not in the shape I was in. So I didn't answer your letter right away, no.'' He added irritably, ''Those eggs are going to be as hard as rocks.''

Jim drained the fat from the eggs and put them on the plates along with some bacon. ''When you didn't answer, I thought you didn't want anything to do with me.''

''That's not true——''

''After all, who needs a stray brother four thousand miles away?''

''I never felt that way, Jim,'' Simon said forcefully. ''I came, didn't I? I'm here.'' He ran his fingers through his hair. ''Look, I know I'm not the easiest man in the world to get along with. I spend a lot of time alone—I have to. But I'm glad we've met again. Glad we're getting to know each other. Just give me time, that's all."

"We've got all summer. If you want to stay that long."

Simon put the toast on the table along with a pot of strawberry jam that had also come from the bakery. This was a moment of decision for both him and his brother, he knew, nor did he minimize the importance of that decision. It was not an opportune time for an image of a woman playing naked in a mist-wreathed lake to flicker into his brain. Shoving it back, he said quietly, "I'd like to stay, yes. You can always kick me out if you get sick of me."

"I'll do that," Jim promised, a smile splitting his pleasant, suntanned face. "Let's eat."

The eggs were not overdone, and there were huge whole strawberries in the jam. Refilling the coffee mugs, Simon said, "I'll get fat if I stay all summer."

Jim shot a derisive glance at his brother's lean length in the chair. "Sure. Anyway, if this dry weather keeps up, there's a way you can lose weight. If you want to."

"What's that?" Simon said lazily. "Canoe races between here and the bakery."

"Fire fighting."

About to laugh, Simon saw that Jim was not joking. "Where's the fire?" he said somewhat facetiously.

"The woods are like tinder right now. We had less snow than normal last winter, and almost no rain all spring. A cigarette dropped in the bracken, a lightning strike—that's all it would take. I'm on the volunteer fire department here, and we help out the whole county. They're running a course next week on ground fire fighting. Want to take it?"

The part of Simon that had felt for months like a lion trapped in a cage said instantly, "Yes."

"Great. I'll sign you up."

"So you spend your winters teaching junior high school and your summers fighting fires?" Simon said quizzically. "That's quite a combination."

"Fighting fires is a breeze after some of the kids I've got. Anyway, I love the woods. If I can save even an acre from burning, that's worth a lot to me."

Every window in Jim's cabin opened into the trees: the drooping boughs of hemlock, the brilliant green of beech, the thin-slivered needles of pine. To think of all these myriad shades of green engulfed in flame and reduced to charred blackness hurt something deep inside Simon. He said with utter conviction, "I already love this place."

"I was afraid you'd hate it here," Jim confessed. "I wondered if we should have stayed in my apartment in Halifax all summer—it's a city, after all, even if it is pretty small beer compared with London."

"I came here to get away from cities."

"But you haven't painted anything since you got here."

Simon's face closed. Fighting to keep any emotion from his voice, he said, "No."

"Well, I sure bumped into the glacier there," Jim said cheerfully and unrepentantly. "I've got to go into town this morning and pick up a few supplies...want to come?"

Town was the little village of Somerville, population seven hundred and fifty. "Not really. I'll clean up the dishes, and then I'll read for a while."

"Once I get back, we should go for a swim—it's going to be another scorcher of a day." Jim reached for the shopping list that was taped to the door of the refrigerator.

Would he ever be able to swim again without thinking of a woman's nude body playing in the water? To his horror Simon heard himself say, "I'd thought there wasn't another cabin farther out than this one. But I saw a place on Maynard's Lake in one of the coves."

"Oh, that's Shea's cabin."

"Shay?" Simon repeated, puzzled.

"Spelled S-H-E-A but pronounced 'shay.'" She's a good friend of mine. You'll meet her sooner or later."

"What do you mean by good friend?" Simon said carefully. Of all the scenarios he had pictured, that the unknown woman might be involved with his brother had not been one of them.

"Just what I say. When I was fourteen and she was eighteen, I was madly in love with her... after all, who wasn't? But by the time I'd got my teaching degrees I'd met Sally, and Shea kind of dropped into the background in any romantic sense." His voice a touch overly casual, he added, "You'd probably like her."

"Matchmaking?" Simon asked, a little too sharply for his own liking.

Jim gave a snort of laughter. "You don't know Shea! She's not into being matchmade. If there is such a word."

Simon did a quick calculation. "So at twenty-nine she's still unattached."

"Yeah. Just like you at thirty-five."

"Anyone ever tell you that you can be decidedly aggravating, James Hanrahan?"

"Sally does. Frequently." Restlessly Jim got up from his chair. "I'll be glad when she gets home. It seems like an age since I've seen her."

Sally, like Jim, was a teacher; they had met in university and had taught together in an isolated outpost on Baffin Island. But Sally had stayed on there when

Jim had got his present job in Halifax, and was only now transferring to a school just outside the city. She was presently visiting her parents in Montreal, and then her sisters in New Brunswick, and would not arrive in Nova Scotia for another month. Jim, plainly, was finding the delay hard to take. "Do you want to marry her?" Simon asked bluntly.

Jim nodded. "If she'll have me. Isolation postings do kind of throw people together, and she thinks we should take the winter to get reacquainted."

"Makes sense."

"Sense doesn't have much to do with the way I feel around Sally. You ever feel that way about a woman, Simon?"

Yes, Simon thought. This morning, when I saw a woman called Shea playing in the lake. "I've never married," he said evasively. "Too busy getting to the top. The women I go out with are the decorative, sophisticated ones that a man in my position is supposed to be seen with. You know, the kind that get photographed in the glossy fashion magazines. Wouldn't be caught dead without at least a quarter of an inch of makeup on. Wouldn't be caught dead without an escort who wasn't at the top, either," he finished cynically.

"Doesn't sound as though you like any of them very much," Jim observed.

"Liking is not what it's about." Simon pushed back from the table. "Hell, I didn't even like myself very much. And that is the last remark of a personal nature that you're getting out of me today."

"Okay, okay," Jim said, slapping the back pocket of his jeans to see if he had his wallet. "Although if you're into that kind of woman, Shea is definitely not the one for you... Want anything at the store?"

"No, thanks."

Simon started stacking the plates, and a few moments later heard Jim's truck drive away down the dirt lane that linked them to the highway. So the lissom swimmer in Maynard's Lake was called Shea. She was twenty-nine years old, unattached, and, if he could trust the intonation in Jim's voice, a very independent lady. Apparently he was going to meet her, sooner or later.

In his brother's opinion she was not the right woman for him.

Or else he was the wrong man.

CHAPTER TWO

AT FIRST glimpse the scene in front of him was one of utter confusion. Simon stood beside Jim's truck in his jeans and T-shirt and new steel-toed boots, taking everything in, and gradually the various components began to make sense. The weather-beaten building on the far side of the road appeared to be functioning as dormitory, kitchen, and command post; two men with sleeping rolls disappeared inside it, and from it wafted the smell of chicken soup. Heaps of gear stood around in the dust: pumps, shovels, chain saws, and big yellow bags of hose. He remembered those long lines of hose from the course he had so lightheartedly agreed to take. Filled with water, they were astoundingly heavy.

From behind the building he heard the decelerating whine of a helicopter engine. Helicopters, he now knew, were used for water-bombing and for transporting ground crew to fires unreachable by road. The truck parked near Jim's had a shiny aluminum water tank, and the volunteer fire truck behind it carried a portable tank. Two bulldozers were lined up farther down the track.

His gaze shifted, almost unwillingly, to the west. There, on the horizon, was the reason he was here.

The smoke was yellow more than blue, a thick, ominous cloud spread over gently rolling hills. He had somehow expected the smoke to be lying still, crouched like a predator over its prey. Instead it was full of roiling movement, billowing high into the sky. Although he was too far away to see flames, the surging smoke alone was enough to make his heart beat faster.

Jim was jogging back toward the truck. "I checked in with the fire boss," he said as soon as he was in earshot. "Four of us are going to do mop-up on the flank that's farthest from the road—you want to take a run down to the helicopter and find out from the pilot how soon we can go? I'll grab a couple of bunks in the meantime."

Glad to have something tangible to do, Simon headed across the dirt road. The dozers had pushed it farther to the west, in a tumble of rocks and earth. Better a helicopter than drive on that, he thought, nodding at three men in filthy orange suits who had just come out of the command post. Their faces were covered with soot, their eyes red-rimmed, and again he felt his heartbeat quicken. London, more than ever, seemed like another world. He was suddenly, fiercely glad to be here. Whatever he was to do in the next twenty-four hours would be real and useful.

More so than putting pigment on canvas.

He went past the corner of the building. The engine of the helicopter had been turned off and the blades were still. It did not look large enough to carry four men and a pilot.

Simon walked around the nose. Someone was balancing on the narrow step that was two feet from the ground, and was reaching into the cabin. With a jolt of surprise he saw that the body in the dirt-streaked beige flying suit was definitely not a male body; the curves under the cotton fabric were female curves, and the waist far too slender to belong to a man. All the warnings of sabotage so liberally posted in Heathrow Airport rose in Simon's mind. He said sharply, "What are you doing here? Get out of that cabin!"

The body went absolutely still. Then the woman turned to look at him. Her eyes the cold gray of a November sky, she said precisely, "I beg your pardon?"

"You heard me—you're trespassing."

In a single lithe movement that brought a frown to his face, so familiar did it seem, she jumped to the ground. "I'm not in the mood for jokes," she said. "What do you want?"

"I came here to tell the pilot that four of us need transport out to the south flank of the fire——"

"Okay," she said impatiently, "you've told her. We can——"

"*You're* the pilot," Simon said blankly.

"I'm the pilot," she repeated, unsmiling. "I'm not in the mood for chauvinist remarks, either."

He had not been about to make any. Although his assumption that a pilot had to be a man was about as chauvinistic as he could get.

For a moment Simon regarded her in silence. She looked tired and dirty and hot. While her hair, tawny blond, was pulled back into a ribbon, wisps of it stuck to her face; there were shadows like bruises under the level gray eyes. Her nose had an interesting bump in it, and her mouth was too generous for true beauty. He wanted very badly to make that mouth smile.

He said straightforwardly, "I'm sorry. I should never have assumed that you had to be a man."

She gave him the briefest of nods. "Okay. We can leave in about half an hour. I have to refuel first."

Turning away from him, she knelt down to unlatch the cargo pod in the belly of the helicopter. Plainly he was dismissed. Yet something in the way she moved, in her slimness and the curve of her back, made Simon say with a gaucheness rare to him, "I don't know your name."

She was hauling a fuel pump from the pod. Resting it on the ground by one of the skids, she brushed her hands down her pants and stood up. She was tall, perhaps five feet nine. He liked tall women. "Shea Mallory," she said.

Shea . . . he could not have come across two women named Shea in the space of three weeks. He croaked, "Do you have a cabin on Maynard's Lake?"

She frowned at him. "Yes," she said in a clipped voice. "How do you know that? I've never laid eyes on you before."

She had not laid eyes on him. But he most certainly had laid eyes on her. Although his heart was banging against his ribs, at another level Simon was not even surprised to learn her identity, for every movement she had made in the last few minutes had told him who she was. Feeling color creep up his neck, fighting to keep his voice casual, he said, "I'm Simon Greywood. Jim Hanrahan's brother." He held out his hand.

Shea took it with noticeable reluctance and gave it the lightest of pressures before releasing it. "The one from England," she said. "The artist."

"That's right," he said, smiling at her in a way a number of women in London would have recognized. "I'm here for the summer."

She did not smile back. Instead she gave his spanking-new T-shirt a derisive glance. "Aren't you afraid you'll get your hands dirty?"

He felt his temper rise. "I did apologize for my mistake."

"I wasn't referring to that particular mistake."

"So what have you got against me, Shea Mallory?"

"I'll tell you," she answered, scowling at him as she thrust her hands in the pockets of her pants. "I helped Jim write that first letter to you, so I know how much it meant to him. His parents didn't tell him he was adopted until he turned twenty-five... once he discovered he had an older brother, he wanted to get in touch with you right away. So he wrote to you. And for six weeks you didn't even bother to write back."

"That's true," Simon said shortly. "But——"

"With all the money you've got, I would have thought you could have picked up the phone—seeing that you were too busy painting rich people to write a letter."

"This is really none of your business—it's between Jim and me, and nothing to do with you."

She raised her voice over the growl of an approaching truck. "He and I went canoeing four weeks after he wrote to you. He was really upset—and he's my friend. In my book that makes it my business." She glanced to her right. "Now you'll have to excuse me—that's the truck with the oil drums. Be back here at quarter-past nine."

The truck lurched down the track and came to a stop three feet from where Simon was standing. The driver gave Shea a cheery hello and climbed out. Simon, knowing he had definitely got the worst of that round, strode up the hill to find his brother.

Jim was standing by a pile of gear chatting to two other men, whom he introduced as Charlie and Steve. Simon said, "We leave at nine-fifteen."

"We've got time for a coffee, then," Steve said, and headed for the kitchen, Charlie hard on his heels.

"Jim, why the devil didn't you tell me Shea was the pilot?" Simon demanded.

Jim blinked. "For one thing, I didn't know...there are seven or eight different pilots. For another, I didn't want to engineer any kind of an introduction and be accused of matchmaking."

"You don't have to worry—she can't stand the sight of me."

"Whyever not?"

"She thinks I should have picked up the telephone the minute I got your letter."

"That's not exactly her business," Jim said thoughtfully.

"That's what I told her. Which didn't endear me to her."

"Oh, well, I suspected she might not be the woman for you," Jim said with a dismissiveness that grated on Simon's nerves. "Why don't we grab a coffee and a doughnut before we go? It's going to be a long day."

Simon subdued various replies, making a manful effort to pull his mind off an encounter that had left him as stirred up as an adolescent. "Won't we need gear out there?" he asked.

"The Bell—the big helicopter—took it out half an hour ago along with another crew. This isn't a bad fire, as forest fires go...a good way for you to get your feet wet."

The fire was not foremost in Simon's mind. He had now seen two sides of the woman called Shea: the laughing creature playing in the water, and the cold-eyed pilot of a government helicopter. Although he was still smarting from her rebuff, this did not in any way diminish his desire to find out more about her. Both sides of her had got under his skin. Nor, he was sure, were these two facets of her personality the whole woman.

Besides which, he was determined to make her smile.

At him.

At nine-fifteen the four men headed toward the helicopter, Simon now arrayed in his orange overalls and carrying his hard hat and ear protectors. The sharp tang of smoke filled the air.

Shea was sitting in the helicopter doing her preflight check. Without making it at all obvious Simon engineered it that he was the one to sit beside her in the front. After doing up his seat belt, he put on the headset, prepared to enjoy himself. The cockpit was small, so he was sitting quite close to her. Unlike the women he was accustomed to, she did not smell of expensive perfume. She smelled of woodsmoke.

She checked over her shoulder to see that she had her four passengers. Then, all her movements calm and unhurried, she flipped a number of switches and opened the throttle. The blades started to whirl, faster and faster, and the cockpit jounced up and down. After waiting a couple of minutes for the starter to cool, she turned the generator on, wound to full throttle and did the last of her checks.

Then her voice came over Simon's headset. "Patrol three to fire boss. Taking off with four mop-up crew for the south flank of the fire. Over."

"Okay, patrol three. The Bambi's out there already. Proceed to the head of the fire for water drops. Over."

"Roger, fire boss. Over and out."

The Bambi, Simon knew from his course, was the brand name for the water-bombing bucket. His muddled feelings for the woman beside him coalescing into simple admiration for her skill, he watched as she eased up on the throttle with her left hand, her feet adjusting the anti-torque pedals. As gently as a bird, the helicopter lifted from the ground, the dust swirling from the down draught. She turned the nose into the wind, picked up the rpm's, and with her right hand on the cyclic drove the machine forward and up. Feeling much as he had on his first plane trip, Simon saw the depot fall behind them, the trees diminishing to little green sticks, the dozer road to a narrow brown thread.

He said spontaneously, "How long have you been a pilot?"

"Four years on helicopters. Three years fixed-wing before that."

As she brought the helicopter around in a steep turn to face the fire, his shoulder brushed hers. The contact shivered along his nerves, much as the ripples had spread over the surface of the lake. Because her shirtsleeves were rolled up, he could see the dusting of blond hair on her arms, and the play of tendons in her wrists as she made the constant small adjustments to the controls. She wore no rings. Her fingernails were rimed with soot.

Why dirty fingernails should fill him with an emotion he could only call tenderness Simon had no idea. Fully aware that everyone on board could hear him, he said tritely, "You like flying."

"I love it," she said. "It's what I like to do best in the world."

The fire was closer now, so that Simon could see its charred perimeters and the columns of smoke shot through with leaping flames. I want to make love with you, Shea Mallory, he thought. I don't know when or where or how. But I know it's going to happen. I'm going to make you laugh with passion and cry out with desire, your cool gray eyes warming to me like mist burning off the lake in the sun. And you'll find there's something else you like to do the best in the world.

Deliberately he leaned his shoulder into hers again, and with a quiver of primitive triumph saw her lashes flicker and felt her muscles tense against his. So she was not as unaware of him as she might wish to appear.

But when she spoke into the intercom she glanced over her shoulder, and her voice was utterly impersonal. "We'll land in that bog to the right of the perimeter—the gear is stashed nearby, and the ground's dry."

She was addressing all four of them, not him alone. Simon's lips quirked. He liked an opponent of mettle. Larissa, his companion of the last several months, would never have reprimanded him about Jim as Shea had, and certainly would never have been seen with dirty fingernails. Larissa was an ambitious young model who had liked him for his fame and money, in turn furnishing Simon with her ornamental person at all the right parties. While the gossip columnists would have been flabbergasted to know they had never been lovers, Simon by then was just starting to acknowledge how badly askew his life had become, and was not about to encumber himself with a love affair. As for Larissa, she was quite shrewd enough to know that the appearance of an affair could be just as useful as the affair itself. Yet the few decorative tears she had let fall at a farewell dinner for him had by no means been fake.

Shea's shoulder twisted against his as she checked the visibility around her. "Fire boss, this is patrol three coming in to land. Over."

"We read you, patrol three. Over."

Again, fascinated, Simon watched the interplay of feet and hands as Shea eased the helicopter down toward the bog. The tangle of alders and tamaracks grew closer and the long green grass fanned out in the wind. The landing was flawless. Over the intercom she said, "Keep low when you get out, and don't go near the tail rotor or the exhaust. Good luck, fellows."

Simon unbuckled his belt, sliding the shoulder harness over the back of his seat. But before he took off the headset he said sincerely, "Thanks, Shea—my first helicopter ride, and with a real pro."

As if she was surprised by the compliment, she glanced sideways at him. A flash of sardonic humor crossed her face. "Hope your first fire goes as smoothly," she said.

He held her gaze. "Do you ever smile?"

She raised her brows in mockery. "At my friends."

"You and I aren't through with each other. You know that, don't you?"

She said gently, "You're holding up the fire crew, Mr. Greywood. Goodbye."

"There's an expression I've picked up from my brother that I like a lot better than goodbye. See you, Shea Mallory."

He got up, bent low because the cockpit wasn't constructed with six-foot-two men in mind, and with exaggerated care laid the headset on the seat. Even though he had had the last word, he suspected round two had gone to her, too.

Why then did he feel so exhilarated?

He swung himself down to the ground. Crouching, he ran beyond the whirling disc of the blades, the wind flattening his clothing to his body, the noise deafening. Two Lands and Forests employees who had been standing near by hurried toward the helicopter, dragging a large orange pleated bucket; Shea raised her machine five feet off the ground and the men, wearing gloves against static, attached the metal cables of the bucket to the belly of the helicopter. When the job was done the helicopter rose into the sky, the bucket dangling incongruously, like a child's toy.

One of the men grinned at Jim. "You have to be careful doin' that—if the cables get caught in the skids, you got a crash on your hands. You guys headin' out for mop-up? Your gear's just beyond that clump of trees. We're joinin' up with another bunch thataway. See ya."

See you, Simon had said to Shea; but the helicopter was now lost in the smoke and his confidence seemed utterly misplaced and his exhilaration as childish as the Bambi bucket. One small word had banished them both. Crash, the man had said, as casually as if he were discussing the weather.

Accidents happen. Helicopters crash. Simon strained his eyes to see through the thick blanket of smoke.

"Coming?" Jim said.

With a jerk Simon came back to the present. Shea, cool, competent Shea, would be truly insulted if she knew he was worrying about her crashing, he thought wryly, and forced his mind to the job at hand. And there it stayed for the next eleven hours. Each man was given a sector to work at the tail of the fire, that desolate, charred acreage where the fire had already passed. Simon dug up tree roots where embers could be smoldering; he chopped down snags; he set fires to burn out the few remaining patches of green; he felt for hot spots in the soil where fire could be burning underground and burst to the surface days or weeks later.

It was a hard, tedious job, without a vestige of glamour. Because daily workouts in a gym in London had been part of his routine, Simon was very fit. Nevertheless, by nine o'clock that evening when the beat of an approaching helicopter signaled the end of their day, every muscle and bone in his body was aching with fatigue.

At intervals throughout the day he had caught the distant mutter of an engine, and had seen Shea's blue helicopter swinging around the head of the fire with its load of water. Now he was almost relieved to see that it was not Shea's small machine but the larger Bell that was sinking down into the clearing near the small knot of men. He didn't have the energy to deal with Shea right now, he thought, heaving himself aboard. All he wanted to do was sleep.

The Bell disgorged them behind the command post. "Great way to spend a Saturday evening, eh?" Jim said, a grin splitting his blackened face. "You okay?"

"Do I look as bad as you?"

"I've seen you look better . . . there's a lake half a mile down the road, we could take the truck and go for a swim."

"Don't know if I've got the energy." Simon groaned. "Is this how you Canadians separate the men from the boys?"

A light female voice said, "It's one of the ways. Hi there, Jim, how did it go?"

"Good," Jim said, and rather heavy-handedly began talking to the man with Shea, a tall, good-looking man in a beige flying suit like Shea's.

Said Simon, "Good in no way describes the day I've had. But you, Shea, look good."

She was wearing jeans and a flowered shirt, her tawny hair loose on her shoulders in an untidy mass of curls that softened the severity of her expression. He added, "That was a compliment. You could smile."

"You're persistent, aren't you?"

"Tenacious as the British bulldog, that's me," Simon said. "How was your day?"

"Great. The fire's under control—got stopped at the firebreak. So now there'll be lots more work for you," she finished limpidly.

Jim and the pilot had moved away. "Unemployment is beginning to seem like an attractive option," Simon said.

"I didn't think you'd stick with it," she flashed.

"I'd hate to prove you wrong."

"Be honest, Simon," she retorted. "You'd love to prove me wrong."

It was the first time she had used his name. He liked the sound of it on her tongue. Very much. What the devil was happening to him? She was an argumentative, unfriendly and judgmental woman. Why should he care what she called him? "If I stick with it, will you smile at me?" he asked.

He saw laughter, as swift as lightning, flash across her eyes. She said primly, "I don't make promises that I might not keep. And I distrust charm."

"I have lots of sterling virtues—I don't drink to excess, I don't do drugs, and I pay my taxes."

"And," she said shrewdly, "you're used to women falling all over you."

"You could try it some time," he said hopefully.

"I never liked being one of a crowd."

His eyes very blue in his filthy face, Simon started to laugh. "I think a woman would have to be pretty desperate to fall all over me right now. I stink."

"You do," she said.

"Hey—you've agreed with something I've said. We're making progress."

Glowering at him, she snapped, "We are not! You can't make progress if you're not going anywhere." Looking around, she added with asperity, "Where's Michael gone? We're supposed to——"

"Is he your boyfriend?" Simon interrupted.

"No."

Until she spoke he was not aware how much the sight of the good-looking pilot at her side had disturbed him. He said indirectly, "I hate coy women."

"You like complaisant women, Mr. Greywood."

"Then you're a new experience for me, Ms. Mallory... Michael's over by the oil drums."

She tossed her head, turned on her heel, and stalked over to the stack of oil drums. Well pleased with himself, Simon headed for the kitchen, and when Jim joined him a few minutes later said, "I could do with a swim—you still interested in going?"

"Sure," Jim said. "What did you say to make Shea look like a firecracker about to explode?"

"I have no idea," Simon said blandly. "But thank you for diverting the estimable Michael."

Jim put a hand on his arm and said soberly, "Don't play games with Shea, Simon. She's not one of your sophisticated types—she could get hurt."

"She's not going to let me get near enough to hurt her." Simon shifted his sore shoulders restlessly. "Let's go for that swim."

CHAPTER THREE

THREE days passed, hot, cloudless days where the wind blew ashes in ghostly whorls among the charred stumps and fanned the flames of back fires. Simon's muscles grew accustomed to the hours of hard labor, labor which he was finding oddly satisfying. There was nothing romantic about mopping up after a fire. But he knew he was protecting the unburned woods from further outbreaks, and that pleased him inordinately. Not even the news on the second day that the fire had leaped the break and was again out of control could entirely dissipate his pleasure in a job as far removed from painting portraits as he could imagine.

Mopping up certainly didn't give him the time or the energy to sit around and brood about his creativity. Or rather his lack of it.

Only two things were bothering him. The majority of the men were holding back from him; and Shea was avoiding him.

As he stooped to pour fuel into his chain saw he remembered the conversation he had overheard in the dark woods by the lake the very first evening he had been here. He had been sitting on the grass doing up his boots when he had heard one of the other swimmers say from behind a clump of trees, "Who's the new guy?"

"Jim Hanrahan's brother," Steve had replied.

"Don't look like a brother of Jim's to me. Speaks kind of funny—like he's royalty."

"He's from England," Steve said.

A third, derogatory voice said, "He's a painter."

"Nothin' wrong with that," the first voice responded. "I've painted a house or two in my day."

"Pictures, Joe," the third voice said. "Pictures that you hang on the wall."

"Oh," said Joe.

"He did just fine on the job today," Steve put in. "You get used to the way he talks after a while."

"Yeah?" Joe said dubiously. "Well, we'll see how long he lasts..."

This conversation had struck a chord in Simon, who had already noticed how some of the crew were ignoring him and how he was always on the fringe of their horseplay; and the next three days merely confirmed that impression. Jim had not been much help. "You're different," he said. "You're a rich and famous artist, totally outside their experience. They don't know what to do with you, so they act as if you're not there. They'll get over it."

As he capped the fuel can, Simon wondered how many more days he'd have to spend mopping up before he was allowed to join their ranks. While it was an exclusion he understood, he could have done without it.

As for Shea, she was spending long hours water-bombing, and Michael did most of the ground crew drops. In her off-hours, whether she was eating, talking, or playing cards, she always seemed to be surrounded by men. As the lone woman in a male environment, the deft way she handled them was admirable. But he was beginning to feel like a large and hungry dog whose chain was too short to reach the feed dish.

He scrambled up the side of a hill to cut down six or seven blackened tree stumps, and half an hour later was on his way back to the base. Michael was the pilot.

Because he was far less tired now than he had been the first day, Simon headed for the command post to check on the fire's progress. The fire boss was talking on the radio, and waved at him genially, and two other ground crew nodded at him. As he bent over the infrared maps he heard Shea's voice coming from the next room. It took him a moment to realize she was using the telephone.

"No, I can't get away—the fire's still out of control. But I'll be off next weekend, because I'll be up to maximum hours by then.

"I didn't promise!

"Peter, I told you when we first met that in the summer I don't have a schedule, I just have to go where the work is. That's the way it is.

"I am *not* married to a helicopter! But this is how I earn my living. Look, there's no point fighting about this—couldn't we meet on Saturday as we'd planned?

"I see. I really hate this, Peter——"

There was a sudden silence, as though the man at the other end had slammed down the phone. A few moments later Shea marched through the room, saying crisply to the fire boss, "Thanks for the use of the phone, Brad."

In one swift glance Simon had seen her flushed cheeks and brilliant eyes. Not sure if it was rage or tears that had given them their sheen, he kept his eyes assiduously on the map. The door swung shut behind her, and as if in sympathy the radio crackled with static. Simon finished what he was doing and went to find his brother for a swim. He hoped it hadn't been tears.

As always, the cool water of the lake felt like the nearest thing to heaven. Afterward Simon hauled on a pair of clean jeans and his running shoes, relishing the

breeze on his bare chest. He angled up the hill to where
he had parked the truck; Jim had been roped into a poker
game back at the base. Eight or nine of the ground crew
were standing between him and the truck, including two
men new to Simon. There was a litter of empty beer cans
on the ground.

"Who's the blonde?" one of the new men asked,
tipping back a can to drain it.

Steve answered. "Name's Shea Mallory, Everett. She's
a helicopter pilot."

"No kidding. She ever go swimming?"

There was a warning note in Steve's voice. "She goes
up at the other end of the lake, and we stay at this end."

Everett was patently unimpressed. "Yeah? Now if I
met her down by the lake, let me tell you what I'd do
to her——"

His string of obscenities fell on Simon's ears like live
coals. Not even stopping to think, he dropped his shirt
and towel on the path. In a blur of movement he seized
Everett by the shirtfront, lifting him clear off the ground.
"You listen to me," he snarled. "If I ever see you within
ten feet of Shea Mallory, I'll drive you straight into the
middle of next week."

"I didn't——"

"Do you hear me?" Simon shook the man as if he
were a bundle of old rags. "Or do I have to show you
that I mean business?"

"Yeah, I hear you. I was only kidding. No need
to——"

His muscles pulsing with fury, Simon grated, "And I
don't want you ever mentioning her name again. Have
you got that, too?"

"Sure. Sure thing."

Feeling the sour taste of rage in his mouth, Simon shoved the man away. Everett staggered, belched, and edged himself to the very back of the small group of men. Into the small, gratified silence Steve said with genuine warmth, "Good move, Simon. Want a beer?"

Simon's heart was pounding as hard as though he had indeed come across Everett mistreating Shea. But he was quite well able to recognize what the offer of a beer represented. He had been accepted. He was now one of the crew. "Thanks," he said, nodding at Steve.

The beer slid down his throat, loosening the tension in his muscles. Joe started telling a very funny story about a firefighter and a porcupine, then Steve described a moose in rutting season who had kept him in the branches of a pine tree for over eight hours. Simon, feeling he had to keep his end up, told them about a bad-tempered stag he had come across when he was sketching in the Scottish highlands, and finished his beer. Declining Charlie's offer of a second, he asked if anyone wanted a drive back to the base. "We're gonna finish up the beer before we head back," Joe said. "Brad don't like us to drink in the bunkhouse. See you later, Simon."

There was a chorus of grunts and goodbyes. Feeling as though he had won a major victory, Simon got in the truck and drove away from the lake. His headlights bounced on the ruts and potholes; the only other light came from the dull red glow of the fire on the horizon, and the faraway glitter of the stars. The trees that crowded to the ditch were blacker than the sky, he thought absently, easing the truck over a ridge of dirt baked hard as stone, and enjoying the cool air on his bare chest. He'd left his shirt and towel behind, he realized ruefully. Maybe Everett would bring them back for him. Then again, maybe he wouldn't.

His foot suddenly found the brakes, his eyes peering through the dusty windshield into the woods. He'd seen a flicker of white move through the trees, he'd swear he had.

It must have been a deer. They had white tails.

But the brief image Simon had glimpsed from the corner of his eye did not fit that of a deer. He let the truck jounce down the hill and around the next corner, and then came to a halt and turned off the engine. After opening the door very quietly, he slid to the ground, and pushed it shut without letting the catch click. Keeping to the grass verge, letting his eyes adjust to the dark, he rounded the corner and began creeping back up the hill the way he had come.

His sneakers rustled in the grass. A bough brushed his shoulder, and a mosquito whined in his ear. The stars were dazzlingly bright. Maybe he'd imagined that flicker of movement, he thought. The fight with Everett had got his adrenaline going and his imagination had done the rest.

He stopped in the shadow of a fir tree, inhaling the tang of its resin, his fingers brushing the living green of its needles. He had seen too many dead trees the last few days, smelled too much smoke...

To his left a branch cracked and footsteps came toward him through the trees. Footsteps that were making no effort at concealment.

All the hairs rose on his neck. He stood still as a statue, scarcely breathing, and saw a slim figure emerge from the trees. It scrambled down the ditch, up the other side, and onto the road.

"Hello, Shea," he said.

She gave a shriek of terror and whirled to face him. She was wearing a white shirt, a small haversack slung over one shoulder.

Quickly Simon stepped out on the road. "I'm sorry," he said, "I didn't mean to scare you. I saw you from the truck—or at least I saw something. I didn't know it was you."

"Do you always creep up on people like that?" she said shakily.

He came closer to her. Her eyes were wide and the pulse was racing at the base of her throat. "You were hiding in the woods," he said. "Why?"

"No, I wasn't!"

"Come on, Shea."

She swallowed, and tried again. "Okay, so I was. I wanted to walk back to the base, that's all. By myself."

"You were swimming?" Simon asked, thinking furiously.

"Yes. Steve gave me a ride up to the far end of the lake, but I told him I'd find my own way home." She looked straight at him, her eyes black like the sky. "I really want to be alone, Simon . . . it's only a ten-minute walk."

He said quietly, "You overheard Everett."

"No!" She caught herself, but not quickly enough. "I don't know what you mean."

"Are you angry with me because I interfered?"

Her eyes dropped from his face to his chest, with its tangle of dark hair over muscles hard as boards, then skidded upwards again. "Don't you have a shirt?" she said fretfully.

"I couldn't hold my towel, my shirt and Everett all at once," he said. "And in the excitement of the moment

I left the shirt back there on the bank. Don't change the subject."

She shoved her hands in the pockets of her jeans, hunching her shoulders and staring past him into the dark woods. "Yes, I heard him."

"He'd had a couple of beers too many, Shea."

"So is that supposed to excuse him?" she retorted.

"Nothing excuses what he said."

In such a low voice that he had to strain to hear her, she said, "He made me feel dirty all over."

She looked heart-stoppingly vulnerable, a side of her he had never seen before. As gently as if she were a fawn he might startle with his touch, he slid his hands down her arms, cupped her elbows in his palms, and discovered that she was shivering. "You're cold," he said, concern for her overriding the urgent need to pull her in his arms and hold her. "Let's go to the truck. I'm pretty sure Jim left his jacket on the seat."

She was now staring at his chin, and he was not sure she had even heard him. "I love my job!" she burst out. "I already told you that—I can't imagine doing anything else. But do you have any idea how hard it is to be the only woman in a world of men—day after day, night after night? I'm the only female pilot in the province. And you saw how many women there are in the ground crew—none. I get so sick of men sometimes!"

"Sick of men like Everett. Joe and Brad and Steve—they wouldn't lay a finger on you."

"I know that, of course I do." She bent her head. "Everett stood next to me at breakfast this morning—he looked at me as though he was undressing me. It was horrible."

She suddenly pulled away from him, scrubbing at her eyes with her fists. "I loathe weepy women." She gulped.

"Oh, hell," Simon said violently. Forgetting restraint, he took her by the shoulders, drew her to his chest and held her, rocking her back and forth. "I'm sorry you overheard Everett, Shea, and I swear he'll never look at you again like that. Not if I'm anywhere in range."

"You did sound fairly convincing," she muttered.

He could feel the tiny warm puffs of her breath on his skin. Fighting to keep his head, aware through every nerve in his body how beautifully she fitted into his arms, he said, "And I'm more than sorry about that stupid mistake I made at the helicopter the first time I met you."

She raised her head, looking full at him, and suddenly smiled, her mouth a generous curve. "I think you redeemed yourself tonight—thanks."

His breath caught in his throat. She had smiled at him, and he wanted to kiss her so badly, he ached with the need. He said huskily, "You're beautiful when you smile, Shea—it was worth waiting for."

Her palms were resting flat on his chest, the imprint of each of her fingers burning into his skin. Her smile faded, and she suddenly pushed back from him. "This is crazy," she said breathlessly. "I don't even like you!"

It was as if she had taken a knife and thrust it in his belly. His lashes flickered. She added incoherently, "Don't look like that, Simon! I——"

He didn't want her to know that she had hurt him. That he was vulnerable to a woman he scarcely knew. A woman, moreover, who could not by any stretch of the imagination be accused of leading him on. "Come on, I'll drive you back to the base," he said, his arms dropping to his sides as he took a step back from her.

She grabbed him by the arm, giving it a little shake, and said in an impassioned rush of words, "What I

meant was that I didn't like you when I first met you
and then there was that whole business of the letter to
Jim. But I do know how hard you've worked since you
got here and I know Everett won't bother me again, nor
any of the others very likely, and I haven't even thanked
you properly.''

He glanced down. Her nails were digging into his flesh.
Her fingers were not long and tapering like Larissa's,
but shorter, and somehow capable-looking. He remembered how, all too briefly, they had lain against his chest,
and in his imagination he could picture them elsewhere
on his body, holding him, caressing him. His loins
stirred. Very deliberately he rested his own hand over
hers, holding it captive, playing with her fingers, and
the whole time his gaze was trained on her face.

Her eyes widened perceptibly. Surrender, pleasure, and
panic chased across her face in rapid succession, before
she tugged her hand free and jammed it in her pocket.
She said with the kind of rawness that bespoke complete
honesty, ''I've never met anyone like you before.''

He said, groping for the truth himself, ''Maybe that's
because you've been waiting for me.''

''Simon, I don't like this conversation one bit! If the
offer's still open to drive me back to the base, let's go.
If not, I'm walking back right now.''

He could not possibly hold her here against her will,
not with Everett's words so fresh in both their minds.
''The offer's open. And I meant what I said.'' And, he
added silently to himself, maybe I've been waiting for
you, too.

She was staring at him so stormily that every instinct
in him screamed at him to take her into his arms and
kiss her until her body melted into his. Gritting his teeth,

he turned away and almost ran down the hill, his sneakers crunching in the gravel.

You're a fool, Simon Greywood. It might be a week before you get her on her own again. A week. Or never.

From behind him, Shea panted, "Slow down! We are not—at this precise moment—on our way to a fire."

He gave a reluctant laugh, waiting until she had come alongside him. "I've never met anyone like you before, either," he said.

She stood stock-still in the middle of the road, her hands on her hips. "I can think of any number of fascinating topics of discussion, Simon. The weather. The safety regulations for ground crew. The flight operational directives for water drops, section seven of the provincial government manual. Even, God forbid, Everett. What we don't have to talk about is you and me. Us. There isn't any us!"

"I don't believe that," Simon said flatly.

"You'd better! Because it's true."

"Close your eyes," he said affably, "and I'll prove you wrong."

Her nostrils flared. "I wasn't born yesterday."

"If there's no us, you've got nothing to be afraid of. I'm not Everett, Shea."

"You're a lot more dangerous than Everett," she said tightly.

"Am I now? But if there's one thing I'm sure about, it's that you're no coward, Shea Mallory. Close your eyes."

She said obliquely, "The phone call that I assume you overheard this evening, there being no such thing as privacy at the base camp, signaled the end of yet another relationship in my life. My job comes first in the summer, and men don't like that."

"To quote a woman I know, I don't like being one of the crowd. Close your eyes."

"I never could resist a dare..." With a loud sigh she scrunched her eyes shut. Very softly Simon stepped closer. Cupping her face in his hands, he leaned forward and kissed her on the mouth.

He felt the shock run through her body. With exquisite gentleness he moved his lips against hers, warming them, wanting only to give her pleasure. He sensed her yielding, then, as heat spread through his limbs, her first, tentative response.

It slammed through his body. One of his hands moved to the back of her head, burying itself in the luxuriant mass of her hair, still damp from the lake. His kiss deepened, fierce in its demand. And for a few heart-stopping moments Shea met him in that new place, looping her arms around his neck and opening to him with a generosity that made his senses swim.

Through her thin shirt her breasts were pressed against his naked torso. He remembered her nude form rising from the lake, sunlight dancing on her wet skin, and with his tongue sought out the sweetness of her mouth.

She wrenched free of him, and over the clamor of blood in his veins he heard her quickened breathing. "Simon, I—we can't *do* this!"

He said roughly, "Kissing you feels more right than anything I've done in the last ten years," and knew his words for the simple truth.

"Please...take me home."

"At least admit there's something between us, Shea!"

"I'm twenty-nine years old, not nineteen, and I know about sex," she said wildly. "You're an attractive man and it's a beautiful night and we're alone...what happened is perfectly natural. Plus it's a very long time since I've been to bed with anyone."

Discovering that he liked that last piece of information quite a lot, Simon said, "The same is true for me."

"There you are, then," she said.

"It wouldn't matter if I'd taken a dozen women to bed in the last forty-eight hours," he said in exasperation. "This isn't just about sex."

"For me it is."

"You've got to be the most argumentative, stubborn and cantankerous woman I've ever come across!"

"Good. Then you'll keep away from me from now on—because I'd sure appreciate it if you did."

Furious with her, yet simultaneously lanced by a pain out of all proportion that she could say such a thing, Simon said levelly, "You don't really mean that."

She raised her chin defiantly. "Yes, I do."

"For God's sake give us half a chance!"

Each word falling like a stone to the ground, she said, "I don't want to. And I've already told you there's no such thing as us. There's just a separate you and a separate me—do you get it?"

Her voice had risen. "You're dead wrong," Simon said harshly. "We could make something——"

"No! Because I don't *want* to. Don't you understand basic English, Simon Greywood?"

"You're making a huge mistake."

"*You're* just not used to a woman saying no."

As he winced at her accuracy, she added with a satisfaction that lacerated his nerves, "See, I was right." Spacing her words, she said, "I want you to leave me alone. That's all. It doesn't seem like a very difficult concept."

Simon looked at her in silence. She meant every word she had said, he thought heavily. According to her, she was deprived sexually, she found him physically attractive, and the velvet darkness of the night had done the rest. So she had also been telling the truth earlier, when she had said she didn't like him. Liking, he had often thought, was at least as important as that elusive emotion called love.

Unable to tolerate her physical closeness, hating the seethe of emotion red-hot in his chest, he rapped, "The truck's parked around the corner—let's go." Without waiting to see if she was following, he set off down the road.

When he climbed in and turned on the ignition she was only moments behind him. He drove back to the base as fast as was safe, pulled up behind Brad's car, and got out. "I'm going to watch the poker game for a while," he said. "Good night."

"Good night," she echoed, and headed for the little room off the kitchen where she slept.

Her hips swung enticingly in her jeans. Cursing under his breath, Simon headed for the dormitory.

Simon and Jim spent the next three days at the head of the fire, in the vicinity of the new firebreak. Simon cut down trees, shoveled dirt in the wake of the bulldozer, and was aware of every single pass overhead that Shea's helicopter made. Watching the small blue machine swing through the smoke was about as close to her as he was getting, he thought irascibly; at the base camp, without ever being obtrusive about it, she was acting as if he didn't exist. Avoiding him as thoroughly as Everett was avoiding both of them.

On Friday around noon the fire reached the break, the flames leaping from tree to tree with primitive hunger, the smoke churning skyward. Simon was on the far side of the road they had made, dousing the woods with a long hose. Because he was next to the gang boss, he was further tantalized by hearing Shea's voice over the portable radio each time she was given directions for the water drops.

The demonic energy of the fire appalled him. The smoke choked him, the radiant heat seared through his clothing, and an ember scorched the back of his hand. But he held his ground, and when, late in the evening, the fire largely burned itself out at the perimeter of the break, he was part of the general jubilation. "You did good for your first fire," Joe said, and when the other men murmured in agreement Simon felt a glow of satisfaction.

At sunset he and Jim drove back to the base along the road the bulldozer had made. "I'll go and check that the relief teams are in for the weekend," Jim said, as he pulled up alongside the command post. "Just think what a hot shower is going to feel like. That and a night in your own bed."

"You mean we can leave tonight?"

"Yeah. If all goes well, we might not have to come back. Why don't you go find Shea? I'm not sure where her car is, but we can drive her back to the helicopter depot on our way to the cabin. She's got the weekend off, too."

Simon did not want to find Shea or drive anywhere with her. But his brother was already pushing open the door to the fire boss's office. Straightening wearily, Simon checked the dining room and the kitchen, and then went outside to the helicopters.

Both of them were surrounded by untidy heaps of gear, and the cockpits of both were empty. Perhaps Shea had already left, he thought, hoping that she had. He rubbed at the tension in the back of his neck. He had always hated dusk, for it was neither night nor day, and everything took on a ghostly air as though its daytime reality had been only an illusion.

He turned to go back to the office, and then he saw her. She was slumped against a yellow hose pack, her head resting on the orange pleats of the Bambi bucket, her eyes shut.

Simon was near his limits both physically and emotionally, and for a terror-stricken moment he thought she was dead. He found himself kneeling beside her on the rough ground without being quite sure how he had got there, and it was not until he was close to her that his eyes, still stinging from the smoke, saw the slow rise and fall of her chest under her beige shirt.

She was asleep. Of course. Not dead.

She was not as dirty as he, but she was far from clean, and there were dark smudges of exhaustion under her lids. He felt a surge of emotion that was, at least partly, compassion, and with it a sharpening of the dull ache of loss he had carried around with him ever since Tuesday night.

He'd been a fool to kiss her as he had, he thought bitterly. An arrogant fool. He'd assumed she'd fall into his arms as easily as a pinecone fell from a tree. Whereas all he had achieved was to drive her away. To negate any possibility that she might have grown to like him.

Sure, he'd aroused her sexually. So what? Probably any red-blooded male could have done that.

He'd lost her. The woman who had played with such delight in a mist-wreathed lake would never be his.

"Shea," he said hoarsely, "we're leaving now."

She stirred, mumbled something under her breath, and pillowed her cheek more deeply into the rubberized folds of the water bucket. With deep reluctance Simon stretched out one hand and touched her on the shoulder. "Shea? Wake up."

Her eyes flew open. "Simon!" she gasped. "I—I was dreaming about you... what's wrong?"

He stood up and said formally, "Jim's ready to leave. He'll drive you to the depot."

She frowned, searching her memory. "My car's at the cabin—the helicopter picked me up there."

"In that case we'll drive you home. Come along."

She gave a huge yawn and pushed herself upright, staggering a little so that Simon reached out to steady her. In the scratchy voice of one only half-awake, she muttered, "When you held on to me in the woods the other night, your skin smelled of lake water."

He dropped her arm as if it were a burning ember. "I could have been anyone—admit it!"

She blinked at the harshness of his tone, and he could see her consternation as she replayed the conversation in her head. "I shouldn't have said that... I'm punch-drunk," she faltered. "Where's Jim? Let's get out of here."

It couldn't be soon enough for Simon.

It was a two-hour drive back to the cabin; Shea talked diligently for the first half-hour, then subsided into silence, her eyes drifting shut, jerking open, drifting shut again. Her head lolled onto Simon's shoulder and her breathing deepened. He put his arm around her, wishing with all his heart that he had never met her.

When they were near the cabin Jim said casually, "You wouldn't mind driving Shea home, would you, Simon?

I promised Sally I'd call her this evening, and it's getting late."

"Of course not," Simon said evenly.

Jim drew up under the trees, his tiredness leaving him as if it were a shirt he was discarding. "It'll be good to talk to her," he said. "See you later."

As he jumped out, leaving the door open, Shea sat bolt upright. "Where are we?"

"Jim wants to phone Sally—I'll take you home."

She scrubbed at her eyes. "Oh. Okay. Go back to the road and turn right."

The road to her cabin was narrow and overhung with trees, skirting the lakeshore. The cabin was at the very end of the road, its sole connections with civilization the light and telephone wires. "You aren't nervous here on your own?" Simon asked noncommittally.

She was reaching over the back seat for her bag, her flying suit pulled taut across her breasts. Simon's eyes flicked forward, staring into the pool of yellow thrown by the headlights. "No," she said. "After a week of base camp, this place is heaven." She reached for the handle. "Thanks for the drive, Simon. Bye."

He waited until she had unlocked the door and turned on an inside light before he drove away. She had not made any mention of seeing him again, and he had purposely not suggested another meeting. Cut your losses, that's what you've got to do, he told himself grimly as the truck racketed between the trees. A month ago you didn't know Shea existed. So blot her out of your life. Because she doesn't want to be part of it. And never will.

CHAPTER FOUR

IT WAS, no doubt, an admirable resolve on Simon's part to stay away from Shea. But by eleven o'clock the next morning he had already decided it was a lot easier said than done.

Jim had met him at the door the night before, his face creased in a huge grin. "Sally's suggested I meet her in Edmonston for a few days' camping before she hits the next lot of relatives. Only trouble is, that means leaving you here on your own."

"Go," said Simon.

"You mean that? You'd have the truck, and I can give you the key to my apartment in Halifax. Seems a bit inhospitable of me, though."

"The only brotherly advice I shall give is that you shower before you go." Simon grinned.

Jim left at seven on Saturday morning, looking rather like a little boy presented with a big pile of Christmas gifts. Simon cleaned up the cabin, did a load of laundry, and made up a grocery list, and behind each of these activities like a dark background lay the knowledge that Shea was within four miles of him and wanted nothing to do with him.

Perhaps he only wanted her because she was unavailable. After all, technically Larissa was far more beautiful than Shea. Larissa had been willing, and he had not wanted Larissa.

But even as he formulated the words he knew they were far from the truth. Somehow Shea in a few inconclusive meetings had found a way into his soul. Yes, he wanted her sexually; he was in no doubt about that. But he also wanted her in ways far more complex and daunting, ways that were outside his experience and that he could only sense intuitively.

Not that it mattered. Because she didn't want him.

At eleven he drove into Somerville to get a few groceries. An elderly woman was leaving the little supermarket just as he approached; he held the door open for her, smiling at her because her eyes were such a snapping brown and her housedress so garish and lively a mixture of fuchsia, turquoise and yellow. She was carrying four plastic bags of groceries.

"Thank you," she said, her smile creasing a face as withered as a dried apple. "And who are you, young man?"

"It's been a long time since anyone's called me that...I'm Simon Greywood, Jim Hanrahan's brother."

"Oh, yes, the artist. From England."

"Right," Simon said dryly. "Can I help you with those bags?"

"You can hold them for me while I untie Tigger. I called him that because he bounces such a lot. My name's Minnie Conover. I live just down the road."

Tigger was a large, hairy mongrel who, once untied from the telephone post, did indeed bounce around his mistress, although never so close that he was in danger of knocking her down. He had the same snapping brown eyes as Mrs. Conover. "I'll carry the groceries home for you," Simon offered.

"That would be very kind. On the way you could explain to me why you and your brother have different last names."

"It's a long story," Simon said, amused by her directness.

"I love long stories," Minnie Conover said firmly. "It's so important to know your roots, isn't it?"

They talked about the need for family history for a few minutes, then Minnie prodded, "Jim Hanrahan and Simon Greywood—were your parents divorced?"

Anything to take his mind off Shea. "Jim wasn't even a year old and I was eleven when both our parents died in a freak gas explosion," Simon began. "My dad was English, my mother Irish. They fought cat and dog and loved each other passionately...I was devastated when they died, and in the manner of an adolescent took to the streets. Vandalism, petty theft—you name it, I did it. We had no near relatives, so we were made wards of the court. Jim was adopted by a Canadian couple, the Hanrahans. But no one wanted to adopt me—twelve years old by then and outwardly, at least, as tough as nails. For the next four years I was in and out of foster homes and in and out of trouble at the same rate."

They had come to a small trailer home, its garden a tangle of exuberant color. Minnie Conover opened the gate and Tigger pranced up the path between massed scarlet salvias and orange marigolds. The old lady said, "You'll come in for tea? I really would like to hear the rest of the story."

Discovering that he craved any company other than his own, Simon accepted with pleasure. The inside of the trailer was as untidy as the garden, and spoke as strongly of a love of life. He helped put away the groceries, then settled down at the tiny kitchen table and went on with his tale, meanwhile drinking wickedly strong tea and eating rather too many butterscotch squares.

"I planned to leave school as soon as I was sixteen. My last term, on one of the days I wasn't playing truant, an old man came to talk to us about art. I wasn't interested in art. So I did what I often did when I was bored—drew caricatures of whoever was boring me and passed them around to the other boys to give them a laugh." Simon smiled ruefully. "I'd picked the wrong man. He marched down from the stage, took one of my drawings, looked at it for a long time, and said that if I was interested in putting my talent to more productive purposes I could speak to him after the lecture.

"In some strange way he reminded me of my dad. So I spoke to him, and the next afternoon he took me to the National Gallery. I'd never been there—art was for sissies, right?—and it was as if I'd entered a world that subconsciously I'd always been waiting for. The upshot was that with his help I eventually went to art school, where I learned to work harder than I'd ever known it was possible to work. At twenty-five I started painting portraits, and by a combination of luck and, I suppose, talent, I made it to the top." He shrugged. "End of story."

"And now you have your brother's portrait to paint," Minnie said ingenuously.

The trailer suddenly seemed too small for Simon. Getting up, he said dismissively, "Perhaps."

"So the story's not done..."

"I don't know how to write the next chapter," he said more stringently than he had intended.

As she topped up her mug with more of the black brew, her eyes twinkled at him invitingly. "Maybe all you need is a holiday. Every magazine I pick up these days has an article about burnout. It's very fashionable to have burnout."

"I can't paint any more!" he burst out. "I haven't lost the technical ability, I don't mean that—but the will to paint has gone."

"When my Arnold died, I didn't garden for two years."

"Was Arnold your husband?"

"That's right...has someone close to you died recently?"

"It's nothing external like that," Simon said. "I could understand it if it were. It's as if there's something dead in me—and I haven't a clue what to do about it." He gulped down the last of his tea, wondering why he had told a stranger things he had yet to tell his own brother. "I'd better go, I've taken up enough of your time. But I'd like to come back, if I may."

"Please do. Let me show you the garden on your way out. I have some beautiful poppies coming into bloom. But we mustn't let Tigger out of the gate when you leave—he likes to chase cars."

Minnie Conover had cheered Simon up; he did the groceries, and was walking past the cash registers when a woman with blond hair as tangled as Minnie's garden came in the door. She gave him a minimal nod of recognition, her cool gray eyes like rain clouds, and vanished down one of the aisles.

Shea.

Feeling his temper flare, Simon pivoted, strode between two of the cash registers, and headed after her. She was standing by the vegetable section contemplating the array of tomatoes and lettuce, her back to him. In a voice he scarcely recognized as his own, Simon said, "You're behaving like an adolescent, Shea. Cutting me dead in the grocery shop is the kind of thing a teenager would do."

Her shoulders tensed under her thin blue shirt. She turned to face him, a tomato balanced in one hand. "You know what? It would give me a great deal of satisfaction to throw this at you."

"Try it," he replied with a wolfish grin. "I dare you."

For a moment he thought she was going to accept his challenge. Laughter rising in his chest, he braced himself to duck. But an arthritic old gentleman who had rounded the end of the aisle called out a greeting to her, and the moment was lost. She stammered something in reply, then glared at Simon. "I live here," she seethed. "It would be all over the village if I threw a tomato in your face, and I can't——"

"Then let's give them something else to talk about." Simon put his groceries on the floor, removed the tomato from her hand and replaced it on the pile, and pulled her into his arms. Her body was rigid, her face a blank mask as he lowered his head and brought all his considerable expertise to a kiss any Hollywood director would have admired.

Shock, resistance, yielding, passion: her reactions followed one another in dizzying succession, and Simon's passion, banishing his anger, leaped to meet hers. It was not, he thought, by any stretch of the imagination a decorous kiss. Certainly it was not suitable for a village grocery shop. And then, enraptured by the softness of her breasts against his chest, he stopped thinking altogether.

A piercing whistle brought him back to his senses. Still holding Shea hard by the shoulders, Simon looked up. A punk rocker worthy of any London street was regarding them derisively as he demolished a bag of chips. Two checkout girls were watching with beatific smiles, and the elderly gentleman with unqualified disapproval.

She said faintly, "I have never been so mortified in my entire life."

"Nonsense," Simon said robustly, "you enjoyed every moment of it."

She took a deep breath, her eyes as turbid as smoke rising from a fire. "If I never saw you again, it would not be too soon," she said with the clarity of extreme rage. "You're the most arrogant, insufferable, thick-skinned man I have ever come across, and it would take an entire crate of tomatoes to express the way I'm feeling right now."

The passion of their kiss was still singing along Simon's veins. With something less than wisdom he said, "Now that we've got an audience, how about an encore?"

Banners of scarlet flamed in Shea's cheeks. "Let go of me this instant," she hissed, "and don't ever lay a finger on me again. In fact, why don't you go back to England on the first plane? I can only assume the women there admire your caveman techniques—but let me assure you that I do not!"

"You're lying in your teeth, Shea."

With an incoherent gasp of frustration she yanked free of him, grabbed two tomatoes without even looking at them, and headed down the aisle that carried dog food. To the best of Simon's knowledge Shea did not own a dog. Feeling better than he had for several days, he picked up his groceries and left the shop.

His exhilaration lasted all the way home. But as he made lunch it began to dissipate. He had done nothing to make Shea like him, and everything to infuriate her. He should have stood four feet away from her and called on all his conversational skills to woo her. Instead of which he had fallen on her like a rabid beast and in the process made her the center of village gossip.

It was not like him to behave so stupidly. The London columnists who had always made much of his suave, man-about-town image would not have recognized him half an hour ago; a woman with tawny hair and unfriendly gray eyes had banished any pretensions he had ever had to suavity. He'd acted like a fool, he thought caustically. A god-damned fool.

If Shea had disliked him initially, she must hate him now.

That afternoon Simon went for a long paddle on the lake, choosing the opposite direction to Shea's cabin. The wind came up while he was out, and by the time he made it back to the dock he was exhausted. He fell asleep on the couch, dreamed very graphically of Shea, and woke with a headache. Lying on his back gazing up at the exposed boards in the ceiling, he felt bleakness settle on him like a thick fog.

It would be a long time before Simon cared to remember the next few hours, hours in which the cant phrase "dark night of the soul" carved its way into his being. He couldn't have the woman he wanted; she didn't even want to talk to him in the supermarket. And the medium through which he had expressed himself for nearly twenty years, his painting, had fled from him.

He didn't know how to do anything other than paint. Since he was sixteen, he had never wanted to do anything else.

Although he went to bed a little after midnight, Simon's sleep was haunted by nightmares. But when he woke up midmorning, he knew that somehow through the long night he had lifted himself from that dreadful slough of despair. He could take a lesson from Minnie Conover, he thought, sitting on the edge of the bed. Minnie had lost her husband, but she still gardened and invited strange men in for tea. He couldn't have Shea, the living woman. But he did at least have the image of Shea ...

Not stopping to think, Simon got up, pulled on a pair of jeans, and started rummaging through the drawers in the old desk near the fireplace. Sitting down on the couch with a pencil and a pad of writing paper, he began to sketch. Three hours later he was surrounded by a litter of drawings, all of them of Shea playing naked in the lake.

If he had hoped that drawing her would exorcise her, he was wrong. It had only bound her more closely to him.

So closely, he thought with a twinge of excitement, that he wanted to paint her. For the first time in months he wanted to put brush to canvas.

His excitement growing, he sifted through the sketches, discarding some of the preliminary ones, putting aside those that said something he had wanted to say about her beauty and delight. Maybe he'd been fooling himself for the last few days; maybe it wasn't Shea herself he wanted, but her image, her kindling of his imagination and with it the desire to transform her into art.

He went outside, took the canoe into one of the coves, and spent another two hours drawing the reeds with their curved reflections, the exquisite white water lilies, and the rough-textured rocks. He'd go into Halifax first thing in the morning and find an art supply shop.

He made himself a sandwich when he got back, because he'd forgotten about lunch, and then started drafting his composition as best he could on the small sheets of paper. The sun sank nearer and nearer to the treeline and the birds fell silent. With the beginnings of satisfaction Simon looked at his final sketch with its impressionistic blending of a woman's lithe body amid curving reeds, lilies tangled in her hair.

And then it hit him.

He couldn't paint a portrait of Shea swimming naked in the lake. Shea didn't know he had seen her that morning. Shea had not given him permission to paint her like this. What right did he have to put on canvas for the world to see an image that had been so intensely private?

None whatsoever. Not even if it meant his salvation as an artist.

All Simon's newfound energy collapsed. He grabbed the sketches, screwing them into bundles and throwing them into the fireplace. Then he lit a couple of matches and tossed them among the papers. Flames curled around the images, blue smoke rising up the chimney. He watched until there was nothing left but charred scraps lying on the ashes of Jim's last fire. Then he went outside and stood on the verandah, staring at the water through the trees.

For Shea's sake he had done the right thing. But it hurt abominably.

Simon had no idea how long he had been standing on the veranda when he heard a vehicle coming down the lane. Coming too fast, he thought absently, wondering who it was and wishing they would go away. A car door slammed and someone ran toward the cabin and up the steps to the veranda.

"Oh," said Shea. "It's you. Is Jim home?"

She was wearing a pretty flowered skirt and a white halter top, her hair tied with a red ribbon, and Simon's theory that he wanted her image rather than the woman herself was obliterated as utterly as the flames had destroyed his sketches. That she was looking distraught he tried hard to ignore. "Jim's away," he said coldly.

She took hold of his shirtsleeve. "Please will you come, then?" she begged. "Please, Simon..."

He pulled his arm away. "What do you want?"

As she pushed a wisp of hair off her face with her free hand, she left a streak of blood on her forehead. "There's an otter on the road between here and my place. It's badly injured, but it's not dead—I think it must have been run over." Her breath caught on a sob. "I couldn't bring myself to kill it. I thought maybe Jim could."

What choice did he have? "I'll come," Simon said, "just wait a second." He ran into the cabin, took Jim's hunting knife from the rack, and went back outside.

Shea backed her small red car out of the lane, then drove toward her cabin until she came to a corner where the lake curved in to meet the road. The otter was lying on the shoulder of the road. "Stay in the car," Simon ordered, and climbed out.

One glance at the animal's crushed hindquarters told him all he needed to know. Dimly aware that Shea had disobeyed him, he steeled himself and cut the otter's throat. Its fur was muddied and coarse, and in instinctive compassion he pulled the corpse into the ditch among the tall grasses.

Washing his hands in the water, he wiped them dry on his jeans. Then he climbed back up on the road. Shea was standing watching him, slow tears sliding down her cheeks. He said evenly, "It was the only thing to do, Shea."

"I know," she gulped. "It was crying when I first found it. It was h-horrible."

Her tears hurt something deep inside him. But when he stepped closer and reached out for her, wanting only to comfort her, she flinched away from him.

Her gesture was the final touch to a day that had lasted far too long. In a furious rush of energy Simon lost his temper. "Let me tell you something, Shea Mallory—I'm sick to death of you treating me as though I'm a combination of Jack the Ripper and an artistic snob! The reason I took six weeks to answer Jim's letter is because my life's fallen apart around me the last year. For the past six months I haven't been able to paint. That may not sound like much to you, but painting's my life, it's what I do best, and all of a sudden I can't do it." He seized her arm, shaking it, his voice rough with emotion. "So when I get a letter out of the blue from a brother I haven't seen for twenty-five years, I'm not about to pick up the telephone and say yes, terrific, this is a great week for us to get together, since I don't seem able to paint I might as well take a holiday. Don't you understand? It was taking every ounce of my energy to go to the studio day after day to try and work—I didn't have anything left for an unknown brother. Not one thing."

Suddenly aware of how tightly he was holding her, he gave an exclamation of self-disgust and let her arm fall to her side. "Hell, I don't know why I'm telling you this. You don't even like me, you've made it all too——"

"That's not true!"

"—clear," he swept on. "But at least have the decency to listen to my side of the story before you...*what* did you say?"

The muscles in her throat worked as she swallowed. "I like you too much, that's what wrong."

Dazedly Simon passed a hand over his face. "Would you mind repeating that?"

"I told you I find you attractive," she stumbled. "You're as different from Jim as night from day. Jim's my friend, he's like a brother to me. You're not like that."

"Right," Simon retorted. "You haven't been to bed with anyone for a while and I'm as good a candidate as the next man. Thanks a lot."

"*Listen* to me!" Shea cried. "You're twisting everything I say. Yes, I want to go to bed with you, you've kissed me, you must know that. But it's not that simple. You're only here for a vacation and then you'll go back to England—so do I have a month-long affair and then say it's been wonderful knowing you, thank you very much and goodbye? I won't do that to myself, Simon! Besides, my record with men isn't great. Sooner or later my job gets in the way and the man's gone faster than you can say 'helicopter'. So I've been trying to keep my distance from you, and if you were under the impression I didn't like you I sure wasn't doing anything to correct that impression."

"Let me get this straight," Simon said, picking his words. "You don't dislike me—we're talking about defense mechanisms here."

"I suppose so."

"Why didn't you *tell* me?"

She raised her chin. "I just did."

"Do you know how I feel right now? Ten years younger and fifty pounds lighter," Simon said exuberantly.

"Simon, nothing's changed—I'm not going to start going out with you, or anything like that."

"But you don't hate the ground I walk on."

"Once I'd met you, I never really did," she said in a low voice.

Simon said blankly, "You're scared of me."

"I'm scared of what you do to me," Shea rejoined.

"So right now I shouldn't be raining passionate kisses over your jewellike face," he said with a wry twist of his mouth. "Not like I did in the grocery shop."

She took an involuntary step back. "Don't you dare!"

Her reaction rather pleased him. He looked down at her skirt. "Heavy date?"

"I was on my way to have coffee with a good friend in the village—Minnie Conover. I'm going to be late. But I'll drive you home first."

"I had tea with Minnie yesterday. I told her my entire life story."

Shea managed a smile. "She tends to have that effect."

"You'd better wash your face at Jim's before you go," Simon suggested.

She hesitated. Then she said awkwardly, "Thank you for looking after the otter, Simon—I could see it bothered you to kill it...I do like you, you know."

He wanted very badly to kiss her. But he was not going to make the same mistake twice in two days. "Let's go," he said.

While she was in the bathroom, he cleaned and put away Jim's knife and scrubbed his hands at the kitchen sink. Drying them on a towel, he went back into the living room. Shea was standing by the couch holding a piece of paper, her face a study of conflicting emotions.

It was one of his sketches.

"Where did you get that?" he rasped. "I thought I'd burned them all."

"It was lying on the floor." Her cheeks flushed, her grey eyes tumultuous, she looked over at him. "You sure have a vivid imagination."

She deserved the truth; it was long overdue. "One morning when I was out in Jim's canoe I saw you swimming—a couple of weeks before we met."

"You spied on me!" she choked.

"You were playing in the water as innocently as an otter, Shea—I didn't spy on you."

She glanced down at the fireplace. "You must have done dozens of these. So am I going to pick up an art magazine one of these days and see myself in one of your paintings?"

"No. That's why I burned them—because I couldn't violate your privacy."

"You made sure you kept one," she said furiously.

He could feel his temper rising again. "I didn't keep it on purpose—I thought I'd burned them all."

"You know what?" she said roundly, brandishing the sketch. "I wish I'd never met you!"

"I've wished exactly the same thing about you," he grated, grabbing for the box of matches on the table. "Now give me that piece of paper and I'll burn it like the rest."

She clutched the sheet protectively to her breast. "But it's beautiful!" she cried. "You can't burn it." And then she blushed scarlet. "I don't mean it's beautiful because I'm in it, that's not what I meant. You—you're immensely talented, Simon."

He didn't want compliments on his artistic abilities. "Shea, I burned all the others. Give it to me."

"No," she said defiantly, "I'm going to keep it."

Breathing hard, Simon said unpleasantly, "It's not signed—so it's not worth the paper it's drawn on."

Shea gave a gasp of pure outrage. "You think I'm keeping it so I can *sell* it? Make money off it? Damn you, Simon Greywood—I take back every word I said about liking you!"

She looked magnificent in a rage, her breast heaving, her eyes flashing. "So why do you want it?" he demanded.

Clearly she was too upset to be anything but honest. "Because you've captured a side of myself that very few people see. And because, heaven knows how, on a piece of cheap paper with nothing more than a pencil you've made something of incredible beauty."

"I don't even know which drawing it is," he said.

She clutched the paper a little more tightly. "If I show you, you won't try and take it from me?"

"You really do have a low opinion of me, don't you?"

"Promise," she said, her mouth a mutinous line.

"There's a cost to it," Simon said recklessly, forgetting all his fine resolves. "You can keep that piece of paper for the rest of your life. In exchange for one kiss."

Her breath hissed between her teeth. "You're nothing but a rotten opportunist!"

"An unprincipled rogue," he agreed gravely.

"It's another dare," she said, "isn't it? But if I say yes, it's only because I want the drawing."

However, wayward laughter was gleaming in her eyes; he loved it when she laughed. "Put the paper on the table, Shea. One kiss, and then you can go and have your caffeine fix with Minnie Conover."

"I should warn you—if indeed I need to—that I'm not known for doing things in half measures."

"Good," he said.

All her movements full of a provocative grace, she placed the sketch on the table, pulled the ribbon from her hair, and shook her curls into a loose cloud around her face. Then she walked toward him, her hips swaying. "One kiss," she said, "that's the deal."

"I didn't specify how long it might last."

"I'm already late at Minnie's and you wouldn't want her worrying. A nice old lady like that."

She was standing very close to him now, her eyes glittering. "No," Simon said without much conviction, "I wouldn't want to worry Minnie." Then Shea's hands slid up his chest to circle his neck and she pulled his head down.

The first touch of her lips told him she was not quite as sure of herself as she might appear. Briefly he left her with the initiative, his heart pounding in his ears; but as her fingers buried themselves in his hair and her mouth warmed to his it was suddenly no longer a game. Pulling her against the length of his body, Simon began kissing her back, stroking her lips with his tongue, drinking deep of the dizzying sweetness of a kiss he wanted to last forever.

Oblivious of anything but his need for her, he drew her hips hard into his, so that she could not possibly have been unaware of his erection, and with his other hand found the yielding softness of her breast under her thin white blouse. And as the scent of her perfume filled his nostrils he knew he would never forget this moment or this woman.

Her breast fitted his hand as though it had been made for him. He felt her whole frame quiver, and murmured against her mouth, "Shea . . . oh, God, I want you so much."

So swiftly that he felt it as an amputation, she jerked her mouth free, and briefly he saw his own reflection in the stormy gray of her irises. "This is why I tried all along to keep you at a distance,'' she cried, shoving against his chest with her palms. ''It happens every time we come near each other. It's madness, Simon—I won't make love with you, I won't! I should never have started this. I thought for once I could keep everything all very nicely under control and I couldn't have been more wrong. How could I have been so *stupid*?''

She was tugging at her blouse to straighten it, her hands shaking. ''There's nothing wrong with what just happened,'' Simon said in an impassioned voice. 'We——''

''There's everything wrong with it—I'm sorry I led you on. I'll never do that again.'' She was looking around her blindly, as if she wasn't quite sure where she was. ''I've got to get out of here,'' she whispered, and ran for the door.

He could have stopped her. But he was quite sure that if he did she would turn on him like a fury. And, he thought, struggling for some kind of reality, Minnie must indeed be worrying by now.

The screen door shut with a bang and a car engine roared into life. She had, he noticed vaguely, left the sketch on the table. He picked it up and looked at it.

Shea looked back at him, eyes drowned with delight, body a slim arc as she reared out of the water; there were lilies caught in the long strands of her hair.

He wanted to see her eyes like that in the act of love; he ached to hold her naked body in his bed.

Because Shea wanted him just as badly as he wanted her. He knew that now. Knew it without a shadow of a doubt.

CHAPTER FIVE

THE next morning Simon phoned the fire depot. Yes, they could do with help mopping up, and yes, the helicopters would be there water-bombing for at least two more days.

Singing to himself, Simon gathered his gear and left the cabin in Jim's truck. He was choosing to interpret it as a very good sign that Shea had run from the cabin last night. She was certainly not indifferent to him. And in the next two days he was going to find out more about why she was so determined to keep him at a distance. Without, he hoped, the entire base camp listening in.

The phone call with the man called Peter had something to do with it. As did her job.

He was assigned to a crew as soon as he arrived at the fire site, and was heartened to be greeted by Steve, Joe and Charlie like a long-lost pal. By some relatively discreet questioning he found out that Shea was in the blue helicopter at the south flank where the fire had not quite burned itself out. He settled down to work, and as always the hard physical labor brought him a measure of satisfaction.

It was eight that evening before he and his crew made it back to the command post. In the bunkhouse Simon shucked off his orange suit and hard hat, washed his face and hands, and went to eat. Back home in a fashionable London restaurant he would have turned up his nose at overdone roast beef, he thought wryly; but not here.

Holding his loaded tray, he surveyed the dining room. He saw Shea instantly, sitting with her back to him at a table with Michael, the other pilot. He made his way toward them, pulled up the chair nearest her, and sat down. "Hello, Shea," he said.

She looked at him as though he were an apparition, and then blushed entrancingly. "How did you get here?" she croaked.

"Jim's truck," Simon said equably, dousing his potatoes with butter. "How's it going, Michael?"

"Just fine," Michael said, glancing from one to the other of them as he drained his coffee mug. Pushing back his chair, he said, "I'll hose down the 'copters, Shea—you finish your supper."

Shea still had a large piece of apple pie and a glass of milk on her tray. Glaring at Michael's retreating back, she said crossly, "Some friend he is."

She was wearing a flying suit, her hair braided into a semblance of order. "You forgot your sketch last night," Simon remarked, tucking into the roast beef. "How was Minnie?"

"You didn't drive ninety miles to talk about Minnie."

"I came to see you."

She put her face close to his and in a furious whisper said, "Simon, I'm not going to have an affair with you. So you're wasting your time."

"I don't think so," he said.

"And we are not going to discuss this any further in a roomful of men who are—trust me—worse gossips than any woman I've ever come across." As though the conversation was ended, she took a piece of apple pie.

"It's almost worth being knee-deep in soot and ashes all day to have food taste this good," Simon said soulfully, watching the curve of her mouth as she chewed.

She gave a sigh of exasperation, resting her chin in her hands. "I hope you didn't burn my sketch after I left."

"I put it on the bookshelves in my bedroom. You can pick it up any time you like."

"I don't think you ever take your mind out of the bedroom."

Some latecomers, Everett among them, were wending their way through the tables toward them, carrying their trays. Simon said honestly, "It's been there a lot since I met you. And now I think we should talk about the weather...I heard there was a chance of showers tomorrow."

Shea caught on instantly. "They've been promising showers for the last week," she said in a carrying voice. "It must be embarrassing to be a meteorologist, everyone knowing how wrong you are all the time." Then her face changed and she gave a sudden yelp of warning. "Watch out, Simon!"

The direction of her gaze and his own sixth sense flung Simon sideways in his chair, and the mug of scalding coffee missed his shoulder by an inch and splashed harmlessly on the floor. He shoved his chair aside and stood up, his temper flaring, for it had been Everett's mug of coffee. But before he could speak Everett exclaimed, "Sorry, Si—I tripped! Glad it missed you."

Everett was not one bit sorry, Simon thought, swallowing his rage. Everett wanted revenge for having been humiliated in front of the men at the lake. Slowly Simon sat down again, watching as Everett bent and picked up the empty mug.

"I'll send one of the kitchen gals to clean it up," Everett said.

As soon as he was out of earshot Shea said trenchantly, "Women should quit cleaning up the messes made by men like Everett. You looked as though you could have throttled him on the spot, Simon."

"It was a possibility," Simon said levelly. "I haven't forgotten the way he talked about you at the lake."

"Maybe the only reason you were angry that evening is because you want me for yourself."

"Credit me with a little decency, Shea! Yes, I want you. But it wouldn't have mattered whom he was talking about. I can't abide that kind of sexual innuendo."

She looked at him thoughtfully. "Sorry, I guess I shouldn't have said that." Playing with her knife, her head bent, she went on, "There's something I want to ask you and it's been on my mind ever since last night. You told me you can't paint any more, that you've lost the will to paint. Yet you did dozens of those sketches..." She looked up, her face troubled. "Did you do them because you wanted to paint me?"

Wishing he'd sat anywhere else in the room, Simon nodded.

"So if you'd kept all the sketches, you might have been able to paint again?"

His fists were clenched around his knife and fork. Visibly trying to relax them, Simon said shortly, "Maybe. Who knows?"

"Have you done any other sketches since you left England?"

"No."

"Honorable's a very old-fashioned word, isn't it? But I've decided you're an honorable man, Simon."

His fork halfway to his mouth, Simon gaped at her. She was serious, he thought, utterly disconcerted. "Don't make me into some kind of plaster saint," he said warmly. "My thoughts are far from honorable when I'm within fifty feet of you."

"Don't joke about this," she said fiercely, leaning forward, her gray eyes very clear. "I could tell last night what the loss of your painting means to you—did you think I wouldn't understand? If I suddenly found out I couldn't fly any more, I'd be devastated. But you chose not to use those sketches because you knew you would have been violating my privacy to do so. I call that honorable."

Simon could think of nothing to say. He put the mouthful of roast beef in his mouth and chewed it methodically, and as he did so a course of action presented itself to him. He swallowed, took a drink of water, and said, "I've never met a woman like you before, Shea. Do you think we could start all over again? Pretend we've just been introduced? The next step would be for me to ask you for a date. An ordinary date. Dinner next Saturday night, for instance. How about it?"

"That's not why I told you this!"

"I know it isn't. You told me because you're sensitive and truthful and you care about people's feelings." He grinned at her, trying to lower the tension between them. "We could sit across from each other in a restaurant in the city and tell each other how marvelous we are."

Looking hunted and unhappy, Shea said, "There's no point, Simon, truly there's not."

"If it'll make you feel better, I promise I won't as much as touch you. Even if it half kills me."

In a burst of honesty she said, "The trouble is, it might half kill me, too."

Charmed, as always, by her capacity to take him by surprise, he demanded, "Then what's the problem?"

"This is a crazy conversation," she said. "Would you believe my friends think of me as levelheaded and sensible? Simon, I already told you why I won't start anything between us. You'll be gone in a month and I'm tired of men leaving me." Producing an unconvincing smile, she added, "But thank you for the invitation, that was nice of you."

"I do not feel nice!" Simon announced. "I hate that word. I want to know why the devil you're so scared of involvement—how many men *have* left you? I won't give you any peace until I find out."

Her smile vanished. "You're pushing me again."

"I'll do whatever it takes. You should know that by now."

Frowning at him, she pushed her chair back and stood up. "I must go and help Michael spray down the helicopters. It's not fair to make him do both of them. See you."

She picked up her tray. Knowing full well he couldn't stop her in front of a roomful of interested onlookers, Simon watched her leave. He was beginning to thoroughly dislike that innocuous little phrase "see you." Because as far as himself and Shea were concerned it seemed to mean absolutely nothing.

The rain the meteorologists had promised did not materialize. Simon worked like an automaton the next day, knowing this was probably Shea's last day at the site, not knowing when he would see her again, his mood as black as the ground he walked on. It was wonderful that she saw him as an honorable man, he thought sourly, adjusting his ear protectors so that the chain saw wouldn't deafen him; but she still didn't want to date him and he still couldn't paint.

So much for honor.

The saw bit into the tree stump, chips flying in all directions. He made a V-shaped cut, then sliced into the trunk from the other side. The blackened tree toppled down the hill.

He wiped his brow with the back of his hand, looking at his watch. Another hour and he could call it quits.

He was working alone on the steep hillside that was his sector. Once he'd finished cutting down the dead trees, he'd have to get help from one of the other men to line up the stumps vertically. But for now he preferred being by himself.

After picking his way over a rocky gully, Simon revved up the chain saw again and tackled the lowermost of a clump of four charred spruce trees, whose needles must have burned like tinder in the flames. Black though his mood might be, he was still able to enjoy the smooth play of his muscles, the pull in his thighs as he braced himself against the slope... too much of his physical activity in the past few years had been workouts in a gym, he decided, testing a sharp-edged rock to see if it would take his weight before he leaned in to the last stump. The chips flew out from his first angled cut.

Afterward, Simon never knew what it was that made him glance sideways for the merest fraction of a second. A flash of movement from the corner of his eye? An atavistic instinct of self-preservation? Through his plastic goggles he saw a large granite boulder tumbling down the slope straight toward him.

He made a frantic leap for safety. The rock on which his boot had been resting shifted, throwing him off balance, and he felt a searing pain in his thigh. The chain saw was ripped from his hand as he flung himself out of range of the boulder. Then his shoulder hit the ground

with a thud that drove the breath from his lungs, and
his wrist slammed against a rock. Dimly he was aware
of a series of cracks and thumps as the boulder rolled
the rest of the way down the hillside.

For a minute Simon lay still, trying to catch his breath.
Slowly, almost innocently, a burning sensation began to
spread through his left leg. He pushed himself up on one
elbow, noticing that the lie of the land hid him from
sight of any of the other men. The hillside was wavering
in his vision. Must be heat waves, he thought fuzzily,
and looked down at his leg.

There was a long tear in his orange overalls; the edges
of the tear were stained red.

Real men don't pass out at the sight of blood, he told
himself. Not even when it's their own. He didn't have a
portable radio, only crew heads carried those. He took
a couple of breaths and yelled Steve's name as loudly as
he could.

From beyond the gully the snarl of chain saws continued unabated; it seemed a supreme mockery that he
should hear, far to his left, the mutter of a helicopter.
All his movements as awkward as those of a very young
child, Simon eased his body out of the top of his cover-
alls, stripped off his T-shirt, and pushed it down on the
wound. The pain made him gasp.

He shouted again, and then again, knowing even as
he did so that to pit his voice against chain saws and ear
protectors was hopeless. But he had to do something.
He couldn't just lie here, losing more and more blood.

The T-shirt was now red as well. Fighting back great
waves of dizziness that made the blackened landscape
swoop and swing before his eyes, Simon dug his elbows
into the ground and began levering his way up the slope
inch by inch.

The first movement made him groan out loud. After that he gritted his teeth, feeling the sweat break out on his forehead and run, stinging, into his eyes. Then his elbow hit a rock that was anchored in the hillside. It seemed an insurmountable barrier, and for what might have been several minutes he leaned back on it, fighting for breath.

Blood, warm and sticky, was running across his knee. He shouted again, but his voice sounded as though it was coming from someone else, someone a long way away.

Grimly he fought back a paroxysm of shivering. There was no reason to feel cold; the sun was beating on his bare chest and the charred earth was warm to the touch. He tried pressing on his shirt to stem the bleeding, but the pain was so intense that he fell back against the rock, shutting his eyes against a new surge of faintness. A roaring filled his ears.

With unnatural clarity he thought, I'm going to pass out. And by the time the crew quits and realizes I'm not around, it might just be too late. What a damn fool way to die...

The roaring was louder. With a jerk he lifted his head, forcing himself to focus on the hot blue sky. Swooping toward him, hugging the hillside, was a small blue helicopter. Shea's helicopter.

He tried to raise his arm to wave at her, but his muscles wouldn't obey him. Then the machine passed directly overhead, low enough to raise a swirl of ashes that smothered the sun.

She probably thought he was just taking a break. When she'd first met him she'd accused him of being unable to handle the back-breaking labor of mopping up. And now she'd been proved right...he was, quite literally, lying down on the job. He closed his eyes again.

Someone was yelling his name. Then a man's body interposed itself between him and the sun, and Steve said urgently, "What happened, buddy? Chain saw, eh? Okay, we'll have you out of here before you know it."

The next few minutes were never very clear in Simon's memory. He was eased onto a stretcher by Steve and Joe and then carried up the slope, a process that hurt more than he would have cared to admit. In a swirl of soot and ashes the blue helicopter came to rest in the clearing, and four men started lifting him into the back. He did remember Shea's face as she twisted to look at him, her blanched cheeks and wide eyes. He wanted very badly to tell her it was nothing serious. But as Steve pulled him into the cabin his injured leg jarred against the doorframe. He heard a harsh cry of agony, and before he could realize it was he who had made it he lost consciousness.

Simon was in his own bed in Jim's cabin; he lay there, trying to reconstruct how he had got there.

He had been flown to the small hospital in the nearest town to Sommerville, where an efficient but rather heartless young doctor had stitched him up and assured him that, despite some initial discomfort and a considerable loss of blood, he would be fine. Stuffed full of painkillers, Simon had then fallen asleep while waiting for an ambulance to take him home. Shea had been there...or had he dreamed her?

He lay still. Night had fallen. A light shining in the living room enabled him to see some of the details in his room: the bookshelves and the calendar with its photograph of a large bull moose in an improbably turquoise lake. By moving his arms and legs he discovered that he still had the use of all four of them. He felt light-headed and very thirsty.

When he sat up, the bed creaked. There was a thick bandage on his thigh, and he was wearing only his underwear. He needed to go to the bathroom. He reached for the crutches leaning against the wall, hauled himself upright, inadvertently put too much weight on his injured leg, and felt sweat spring out on his face. One of the crutches banged against the chair leg, the scrape of wood on wood excruciatingly loud. Grunting with effort, Simon began negotiating the narrow passageway between the chair and the dressing table. Then he heard footsteps hurry across the floor and Shea walked into the room. He said blankly, "I've died and gone to heaven."

"You have not," she said severely.

He rubbed at his forehead with his good hand, wishing the top of his head would reconnect with the rest of him. "Then it's Saturday night and you've come to pick me up for a dinner date."

"Simon," she said, a faint smile breaking through the strain on her face, "if we ever have a dinner date I promise I won't be wearing one of Jim's old T-shirts. Where are you going?"

He looked her up and down, taking his time. Jim's shirt was too wide for her, but not too long; her legs were distractingly slender, her feet high-arched. "Well, if it's not heaven, it's pretty close," he said. "I'm heading for the bathroom—sorry I woke you, I haven't got the hang of these things yet."

As he rather inexpertly negotiated the few feet between his bedroom and the bathroom, Shea hovered around him, a worried frown on her face. She looked,

Simon thought, less like a competent helicopter pilot than like a mother hen whose chick had strayed. He said, "You wouldn't feel like making a cup of tea, would you, Shea? And could you find a shirt and a pair of shorts in my bedroom?" He gave her a faint grin. "You should take your sketch while you're there—I'm in no shape to do a darn thing about it."

He was in the living room by now, and the light was shining full on Shea's face. As she nodded, her head ducked low, he said sharply, "What's wrong? Are you all right?"

The loose cloud of her hair hid her face. "Of course," she said in a muffled voice. "I'll go and make the tea."

Nearly overbalancing, Simon grabbed her elbow. "Look at me."

When she glanced up, there were tears streaking her cheeks and her lips were trembling. His heart dissolving in an emotion totally new to him, Simon said, "Come here—damn these crutches!"

"You're much too dictatorial," she said querulously, and walked straight into his embrace, wrapping her arms tightly around his waist. She was crying openly now, her words running into one another. "I was so frightened when I saw you lying on the ground—I knew it was you right away. And then you passed out and there was blood all over the back of the helicopter. . . it was awful."

Simon buried his face in her hair, smiling foolishly at the floor. This was not the speech of a woman who disliked him. Abandoning the crutches to their fate, he pulled her close and held her with all the strength he could muster, all the while aware of her tears sliding down his chest. "Why did you fly over that way? You were doing water drops on the other flank."

"I don't know," she wept, "and that's what scares me. I just had this feeling that I should take a look where you were working. I wish I knew what was going on..."

He rubbed gently at the tension in her shoulders, and wondered if it was possible to pass out from sheer happiness. "I'm glad you did take a look," he said. "Sweetheart, don't cry, it isn't——"

She looked up, her eyes flooded with tears. "I'm not your sweetheart, I'm not anybody's sweetheart!"

"Then there must be something badly wrong with Canadian men," Simon pronounced. "What do they do, hibernate all winter and go fishing all summer? Shea, I love the way you're holding on to me, but in all honesty I can't stay upright much longer."

She suddenly seemed to realize how hard she was clutching him. Blushing scarlet, she let go and stepped back, taking a swipe at her wet cheeks with the back of her hand. "I'll go and make the tea," she mumbled, and fled to the kitchen. Simon went to the bathroom.

As he was leaving it to go back to the living room, he made the mistake of looking in the mirror. He looked like a character in a seedy thriller, he thought, rubbing at the stubble of beard on his chin. His eye sockets were dark-circled and his skin, under his tan, was a dirty yellow. If he were Shea, he'd run a mile.

She tapped on the door. "Here are your clothes," she said, and passed them to him. Putting on his shirt was no problem, but it was the work of several minutes to get into his shorts. The painkillers appeared to have worn off.

"The tea's made," Shea called.

Simon splashed some cold water on his face, which made no noticeable improvement, and opened the door. Shea said, shocked, "Simon, you look dreadful!"

"We could have the tea in bed," he suggested, propping himself up on the doorframe.

"*We*?"

"Yes, we. Shea, I'm not convinced I can make it back to the bedroom right now, let alone seduce you when I get there. Unfortunately, I also seem to be wide-awake."

"So am I." She gave him a shy smile. "Okay."

He had half expected her to refuse. Concentrating on putting one foot in front of the other, he made it back to the bedroom and collapsed on the bed, hearing his breathing rasp in his ears. He took off his shirt, propped up the pillows, and got into bed. He was quite sure he could feel every single stitch in the gash on his thigh.

Shea followed him into the room, passed him a mug of steaming tea, and perched herself on the far end of the bed, her legs tucked underneath her. "Shea," Simon said deliberately, "are you a virgin?"

"Really, Simon, what kind of a question's that?"

"Just answer it."

"No, I'm not!"

"Then stop behaving like one. At least sit near enough that I can see you."

She scowled at him. "I've taken a helicopter into places I probably shouldn't have, I've forded mountain streams and been crew in a capsized yacht—but you scare me more than any or all of the above."

"Right now I couldn't swat a fly." He patted the side of the bed. "Come here...please."

In one of those lithe, graceful movements that always made his heart turn over, she got up, walked the length of the bed and sat down again, so close that he could see the bounce of her breasts under the loose T-shirt. His mouth suddenly dry, he said, "I don't know why you came looking for me yesterday. But you got me out of a bad situation—thanks."

Almost perceptibly she relaxed. "What happened?"

He hadn't needed to give that much thought. "Between you and me—because I'm sure I can never prove it—I think Everett got his revenge." Briefly he described the boulder that had so mysteriously tumbled down the hillside just as he had started cutting down one of the trees.

Shea sat up straight. "But you must tell the police."

"You think they're going to find fingerprints on a granite boulder? Don't you worry—I'll get him sooner or later."

"I'd rather have you as a friend than an enemy," she said feelingly. "I'm sure he spilt that coffee on purpose, Simon."

"I'm sure he did, too." Not altering his tone of voice, Simon went on, "The man—or men—you've had love affairs with, Shea—couldn't they take the pressure of your job?"

She plunked her mug on the bedside table. "It's years ago now and I really don't want to talk about it."

Her body was silhouetted against the light from the living room, and Jim's T-shirt was thin from many washings; the shadowy outline of her breasts made Simon want her so badly that he had reached out and taken her by the wrist before he knew what he was doing. "There's something between us, Shea," he said roughly. "You know that as well as I do. I swear I've never felt this way about a woman before. I don't know what's going on any more than you do, and I have to know why you're so scared of me."

"You promised you wouldn't touch me!"

He looked at his fingers circling her wrist as if he was not sure whose fingers they were; then, trusting his emotions, he drew her palm toward him and rested his lips against it in a gesture of inexpressible tenderness, his eyes closing. Her skin was soft, and smelled of old-fashioned lavender soap.

"Simon..."

There was a catch in her voice. When he glanced up, her face was open to him, all the fire in it gentled to simple wonderment, her lips parted. Ignoring the pain in his leg, Simon drew her closer with his free hand and kissed her mouth with the same tenderness, trying only to give her pleasure and to allay her fears. She yielded to him as a reed bent to the wind that blew over the lake, her body seemingly boneless, a supple curve of warm flesh. Then her weight was lying across him on the bed and her lips were moving over his in a tentative exploration that made his senses swim.

He fought for control, afraid that the slightest wrong move would make her shy away like a deer frightened in the forest; through a haze of delight and longing, words rose to the surface of his mind. I'm falling in love with you, he thought. Maybe that's why this feels so new and so different...

Her hands were cupping his face, her hair falling like a sweet-scented mist over the pillow. Then in a hot tide of desire Simon felt her tongue slide the length of his mouth. He opened to her, his loins springing to life in a way that made nonsense of all that had happened to him in the last twelve hours. He could feel his control slipping from him, usurped by the primitive paean of his sexuality, and struggled to hold on to it, to leave Shea with the initiative when all he wanted to do was crush her with his weight and drive into her body with all his strength.

He let his hands drift down her back, seeking out the firm arch of her rib cage and the long valley of her spine. Then, inevitably, he found the edge of her shirt and beneath it the smooth, silky flare of her bare back. The feel of her skin intoxicated him, driving away caution. His tongue met hers in a fierce dance of passion and his hold tightened, clasping the swell of her hips and pulling her hard to his own body under the thin covers.

He groaned deep in his throat as his other hand found the fullness of her breast; it was smooth as ivory, but warm as ivory was not, and alive to him. For Shea, he realized with dawning joy, was both surrendering to him and giving of herself, the lissom grace of her embrace as far from fear and resistance as it could be. Between fast, urgent kisses he whispered her name in passionate gratitude, and felt her mouth leave his to caress the taut lines of his throat and then bury itself in the dark, tangled hair on his chest.

Beneath her palm she must have felt the heavy pounding of his heart. She raised herself on her elbows so that he could see her face; he took her breasts in his two hands, stroking them to the tips that hardened to his touch, watching her eyes darken and her face convulse with the intensity of her pleasure. She gave a tiny whimper of delight, and with it went the last of Simon's control. He tugged at her shirt, drawing it up her body and baring her breasts to his sight. With a smile of mingled pride and shyness that he found infinitely touching, Shea hauled the shirt over her head and dropped it to the floor.

He knew her well enough to know something of what that gesture implied, because for Shea it would not be

a casual gesture; and for the first time in his life he gained
an inkling of what falling in love might mean. He said
huskily, "You're so generous...and so incredibly
beautiful."

For a moment her shyness won. Her lashes hiding her
eyes, she faltered, "I wanted you to see me. You already
did, at the lake, I know—but this time was my choice."

He drew her closer, burying his face in the cleft between her breasts, then letting his mouth roam the firm,
swelling flesh and tight nipples until she was crying out
as a wild bird cried. He pulled the covers down to his
waist, wanting to feel her softness against his chest, their
mouths joining in a kiss as wild as the fire that leapt
from tree to tree.

But in her urgent need to be closer to him Shea forgot
to be careful. As she shifted her knee to keep her balance,
she struck his injured thigh. Desire was eclipsed in a pain
so red-hot, so all-encompassing that Simon might as well
have fallen into the very heart of the fire. His choked
cry of pain sounded shockingly loud; teeth bared, fists
clenched, he gasped for breath.

In a move that had none of her usual grace Shea
scrambled off him. "Oh, Simon, I'm so sorry—I didn't
mean to hurt you." She grabbed for her shirt and wiped
the sweat from his brow, and as the red mist of pain
slowly cleared he saw that she was appalled.

"It's okay," he muttered.

She brought his hand to her cheek. "I wouldn't have
hurt you for the world—you know that, don't you?"

He was breathing more normally now, although his
thigh was throbbing diabolically. And the pain had
brought with it a return to sanity. "It was an accident,
Shea," he said with attempted lightness. "And maybe
just in time. Are you on the Pill?"

"No," she said in dismay, "of course not."

"Then I have to go to the chemists before we make love," he said.

"Drugstore," she corrected automatically. "I never even thought of that."

He managed a smile. "Neither, in the heat of the moment, did I." He patted the bed on the side of his good leg. "Put on your shirt and lie down beside me."

She looked down at the crumpled T-shirt she was holding as though she had never seen it before. "I would have made love with you without even thinking about any of the consequences," she whispered. "I've never behaved like that in my life."

"So don't ever again tell me there's nothing between us," he said forcefully. "We both know the truth now."

Her eyes flew to the door in a small, telling move. With all his willpower behind his words Simon added, "You can't run away—it's too late for that."

She pulled her shirt over her head and flipped her hair back, her gaze flickering around the room like a trapped animal's. "Do you believe me?" she said abruptly. "That the way I behaved tonight isn't the way I normally behave? Or do you think I get into bed with every man who asks?"

"I believe you," Simon replied with careful precision. "For one thing because I think you make a habit of telling the truth. And secondly, because I think at some point in your life you've been very badly hurt. By a man. Am I right?"

She nodded unhappily. The light slanted across her face, shadowing the hollows under her cheekbones and making deep pools of her eyes. "I guess I do have to tell you about it. Because it wasn't just once, it was twice."

"Was one of them Peter?"

"No, he and I only dated a few times." She paused, collecting her thoughts. "You see, my mother died when I was very young, and my father brought me up. He thought I could do anything I wanted to, so I grew up believing that, too. When I was thirteen we visited some relatives in a remote area of northern Alberta. We flew in by bush plane—and that was when I knew I wanted to become a pilot. I met Tim at flying school, when I was twenty-one."

Pleating the hem of the sheet in restless fingers, Shea went on, "We fell in love. It seemed like a match made in heaven, because he was as crazy about flying as I was. Isn't that what all the magazines advise—choose a mate with similar interests?" Her voice edged with bitterness, she said, "Well, it didn't work out that way. We both got our licenses, and right away I got the offer of a wonderful job here in Nova Scotia. But Tim wanted to go to Ontario. Better for his career. I could choose, he said, between him and the job. Between his career and mine. So I did."

"You took the job."

She nodded. "I flew fixed-wing for three years and all that time I was pretty wary of men. Dated a fair bit, but didn't let anyone close to me. Then I was accepted into the helicopter training program. It cost a lot of money and I had to work very hard, but I loved every minute of it. Two years later I met Nicholas out at the airport. He was a lawyer for a major charter company, and we hit it off right away. I was a little more cautious this time, but he was so much in love with me and he understood the demands on a pilot, or so I thought— so we moved in together and started planning the wedding."

Her fingers had stilled; she was talking more to herself than to Simon. "We had five wonderful months. But once summer came my schedule went haywire—it usually does. Nicholas loved to sail, and he always wanted me to go with him. But often I couldn't. And we couldn't plan a summer holiday the way normal people do. We started fighting, then making up and promising to do better, then fighting again." She gave a humorless laugh. "We lasted well over a year and I suppose I should be grateful for that. But the second summer he found another woman to crew for him, a teacher who had all summer off. In August I found out that she was doing more than crew for him." Her voice faltered. "I was shattered. Because I'd trusted Nicholas, you see."

"Rotten bastard," Simon said economically.

She glanced up, blinking a little at the expression on his face. "That was a year and a half ago and I haven't got seriously involved with anyone since him. Peter and I were just dating casually. But even he was the same old story—a liberated woman's fine until a man gets inconvenienced." She ran her fingers through her already disordered hair and said with the same single-minded intensity she had brought to their lovemaking, "I always thought I could have it all, Simon! My job, which I adore. A man whom I love and who loves me. And children too, some day. Am I out of my mind? Or is that possible?" Not waiting for him to answer, she added gloomily, "When I say I want all that, I'm called selfish by an awful lot of people—male and female. But men aren't considered selfish if they want a career and marriage and children. Are they?"

Her job. A man who loved her. And children. Simon lay very still, feeling as if a dozen granite boulders had suddenly fallen on him. What she wanted seemed eminently reasonable to him. And, he thought numbly, had he met Shea a year ago he would have called himself a perfect match for her. He was an artist, with enough of a reputation built up that he could live anywhere in the world and choose his hours of work. Her work schedule wouldn't have mattered to him at all; he could have adjusted to it all too easily. In fact, it would have suited him fine. He had always needed time alone.

He didn't know whether he loved Shea; he did know she led him into unknown territory simply by being herself, and that the feelings she aroused in him were stronger and more imperative than any he had ever experienced before. And the thought of holding in his arms the child he and Shea had brought into being filled him with a bittersweet longing.

A longing he could not fulfil.

A new pain was spreading through his body, one that had nothing to do with his injured leg. He was wasting his time even thinking about Shea. In the last year he had lost his livelihood and all the meaning it had carried for him; he couldn't paint. He had no work schedule that might have fitted in with hers, and the only thing he knew how to do—other than mop up forest fires—was paint.

He was, to put it bluntly, unemployed.

Shea was tugging at his arm. "Don't look like that!" she said frantically. "Is your leg bleeding again? What's the matter? Answer me, Simon!"

With an attempt at normality that took the last bit of his strength Simon said, "No, it's not bleeding. But I could do with another of those painkillers, Shea—they're on the bureau."

How could he tell her what he had been thinking? Worse, how could he possibly have an affair with her? He was nothing but an out-of-work artist.

When she handed him the pill, he said heavily, "Sorry, I seem to have run out of energy."

She was a woman whose emotions were clearly written on her features; Simon hardened his heart against the anxiety and confusion he saw there, and swallowed the pill. She said, "I shouldn't have talked so much...I'll be in Jim's room. You'll call if you need anything?"

He nodded, making no move to touch her or kiss her good-night. She made the smallest gesture toward him, then withdrew her hand, her face full of bewilderment. Simon lay back on the pillows and closed his eyes, and heard her leave the room. A few moments later the light went out in the living room and the springs creaked in Jim's bedroom.

He felt as though something inexpressibly wonderful had been held out to him; but just as he was about to take it, it had been snatched away.

He wanted Shea. But he couldn't have her.

CHAPTER SIX

SIMON slept badly. In his dreams he painted a whole series of nightmarish canvases which began swirling around him in the studio, smothering him in burnt umber and lampblack. He woke to sunshine and birdsong and the small sounds of Shea moving around in the kitchen. She must be getting ready to go to the depot, he thought with deep relief, and lay still, waiting for her to leave.

The screen door opened and shut. Then he heard the slow, rhythmic squeak of the rocking chair on the veranda. When he looked at the clock he saw it was past ten; so she wasn't going to work. Knowing he had to face her sooner or later, he got up, cleaned himself up in the bathroom and hobbled out to the door that led from the kitchen to the veranda. Shea said brightly, "Good morning."

She was wearing her flying suit. "Aren't you late for work?" Simon asked pointedly.

"Day off. Now that you're up, I'll take a run to my place and get some clothes. Jim will be back tomorrow, so I'll stay here until then...I left a message for him with Sally's sister while I was waiting for you at the hospital." She opened the door and walked past him to get another cup of coffee; the scent of her hair wafted to his nostrils, tantalizing him unbearably.

Quite sure he could not endure twenty-four hours in her presence, Simon said brusquely, "I'm a lot better today—I don't need a nursemaid, Shea."

94

She said carefully, "I was thinking more of keeping you company. As a friend."

It was the first time that word had been used between them. He poured himself a glass of juice. "I'll be fine on my own."

She banged her coffee spoon on the counter with more force than was necessary. "What's going on, Simon?" she demanded. "Last night you couldn't wait to get me out of the bedroom and now you're acting as if I have some kind of unmentionable disease. What's your problem?"

"I've managed without a mother since I was eleven," he said unpleasantly.

Her eyes brilliant with rage, she said, "I have never once pictured myself as your mother."

"I'm thirty-five years old, Shea—I can look after myself!"

Her fingers gripping the edge of the counter so hard her knuckles were white, she said, "You didn't like me telling you about Tim and Nicholas."

Worse and worse. "I'm glad you told me," he said shortly.

"Then how have I offended you? It must be something to do with them. I'm twenty-nine, Simon. Would you expect there to have been no men in my life until you came along?"

"It's nothing to do with Tim or Nicholas!" he roared.

"Then why aren't you the same man you were last night?" she flashed back. "You've gone somewhere... a long way away."

He should have remembered that this was Shea, not Larissa. Shea had sensed his retreat, and was confident enough of her own worth to challenge him on it. Discovering in himself a strong prohibition against fobbing her off with a lie, he said flatly, "It's nothing you did or said, I swear. Other than that, I don't want to talk about it."

"Oh, that's wonderful," she said sarcastically. "One minute we're practically making love and the next minute you can't wait to get me out of the bedroom, and I'm not even supposed to talk about it? If that's the way you operate, it's a damn good thing we didn't make love."

Her flushed cheeks and tumbled hair made him want to seize her in his arms and kiss her to silence. And with each word she spoke he could feel himself pulled more strongly toward her; for there was something wild and untamed about Shea that answered his deepest needs. Life with her would never be dull, he thought with a painful twist in his guts. "That's the way I operate," he said in a level voice.

"I don't believe you!"

His strategy fell neatly into his mind. If he made her angry enough, she would leave. And then he could lick his wounds alone. He said, "Shea, last night I was high as a kite on painkillers and you were half naked and I got carried away—you've slept with men before, you know what the score is. But it's morning now, and I'm sober as the proverbial judge. I think it would be in the best interests of both of us if you left."

She sputtered, "You're the one who's been telling me all along that whatever was between us wasn't just sex. Why have you changed your tune, Simon?"

"All along I was kidding myself," he drawled. "Typical male ploy. Surely you've come across it before?"

She had gone white with rage. "Call a spade a spade, why don't you? You weren't kidding yourself—you were lying to me."

"All right, so I was!" he grated. "So why don't you take the hint and get the hell out of here?"

Her voice as brittle as broken glass, she said bitterly, "It's not Nicholas who was the rotten bastard—it's you."

She slammed her coffee cup into the sink, brushed past him, and ran out of the door and down the steps. Her car engine roared to life. Gravel spitting from under her tires, she backed out of the driveway. Then silence fell, and with it the soft sigh of the wind in the trees and the splash of the lake against the shore reasserted themselves.

Simon put his glass down on the counter, feeling exhaustion wash over him. Shea was gone.

That was what he had wanted, wasn't it?

Simon slept the rest of the morning, a deep, dreamless sleep. When he woke up early in the afternoon, several things were clear to him. Shea was in his blood, his bones; he had to have her, without even knowing what those words meant. Which meant he had to get back to his painting.

He got up, showered, shaved, and dressed, operations which took longer than usual because his leg was still very sore. Then with some difficulty he dragged the desk into the light and sat down with a pad of paper and a couple of pencils, and began to sketch. He tried to re-create the granite outcrops and misty reflections of the lake; he outlined Jim's face in a dozen different moods; he struggled with the blackened landscape and writhing smoke of the fire. But again and again, as if he had no will of his own, he found himself drawing Shea: her face drowned in desire, the curve of her shoulder, the flash of her laughter.

He could not—would not—paint Shea.

He did a series of sketches of himself and Jim, two brothers reunited after a lifetime apart. Putting down his pencil, he stared at them. Oh, they were competent enough. More than competent. But there was no soul in them, no spark. They were dead. As, he thought with coruscating honesty, the last of his portraits had been.

His drawings of Shea were not dead. They sang with life.

Furious with himself, he began screwing the sketches into bunches and throwing them into the ashes in the fireplace; and as he was doing so the kitchen door opened quietly. His heart gave a great thump in his chest as Shea stepped in the room. He said in a hostile voice, "Where did you come from? I didn't hear the car."

"I brought my canoe."

She was wearing green shorts and a brightly patterned shirt, her hair in a ponytail that made her look about sixteen. "Then why don't you paddle right back where you came from?"

She winced. But she said steadily, "Simon, that trick worked once, but it won't work again. You manipulated me into getting so angry this morning that I'd leave, didn't you?"

He should have realized she was too intelligent to have been so easily deceived. He said nastily, "It took you this long to figure that out?"

"Why, Simon? That's what I want to know."

He pulled himself to his feet. "Don't Canadian women realize when they're not wanted?"

Her struggle to control her temper was all too visible. "If I thought I wasn't wanted I wouldn't be here," she said with icy composure. "We nearly made love last night, Simon—I take that seriously, and unless I'm way off base I think you do, too."

He did. Of course. The evidence that he did was strewn all over the fireplace.

In a surge of compassion he saw that despite her brave words she was clutching the edge of the counter with taut fingers, her back braced against it. So Shea was afraid, and had confronted him anyway. Yet another strand added itself to the ties binding him to her; with deep relief he spoke the truth. "It was brave of you to come back," he said.

"Brave or insane. Because there's more, you see." She bit her lip. "Your accident yesterday really scared me—we skate on thin ice, don't we? So I—I've changed my mind, Simon. If you still want to have an affair with me, I will."

Into the sudden silence a blue jay screeched in the pine tree by the veranda. The irony of her offer was almost more than Simon could bear. Yet unwittingly she had given him the perfect cue to tell her that he, too, had changed his mind. He said, "Have an affair and damn the consequences? What about Nicholas and Tim and Peter—all those men who've left you?"

Her lashes flickered. "I can look after myself. My dad said I can do anything—so I'm sure I can have an affair with you this summer and stay uninvolved emotionally. That way I won't get hurt."

He didn't like her reasoning one bit. "It sounds as cold-blooded as two frogs mating in a pond."

She smiled, walking over to him and running her fingertip lightly along the inner curve of his arm. "I don't think an affair between you and me would ever be cold-blooded."

Steeling himself against the featherlight warmth of her touch, Simon said, "Then it sounds as if you're using me."

"A lot of relationships are a kind of mutual using, wouldn't you say? We're just being honest about it."

He thought of himself and Larissa; and said sharply, "I may have done that in the past—used women. But you're different, Shea. I can't label what it is I feel for you . . . but I'm certainly not uninvolved."

"I'm sure you're experienced enough to look after yourself," she retorted. "Because those would be my terms."

He shifted his weight to his good leg. How the gods must be laughing, he thought. Because he was going to turn down Shea's offer.

She blurted, "Do you think I'm cheap for talking the way I have? I'm trying not to get hurt again, Simon, that's all."

"I don't think you're cheap, Shea—although I do think you're wrong, no matter what your father said. But none of that matters." He looked around for a chair and eased himself into it, wincing as he bent his left knee. "In the middle of the night you talked about wanting it all—job, husband, children. All I want is you. I can't go further than that for now. But what I realized last night before I kicked you out was that I haven't got anything to offer you. Nothing. Basically, I'm an artist who can't paint, and in my books that makes me a pretty poor bargain. Oh, yes, I own a house in London and a cottage in Sussex and I have a very respectable bank account. But I've lost touch with the only work that means anything to me, and until I can sort that out I have to keep away from you."

Her jaw dropped. "You mean *you've* changed *your* mind?"

"I have to be able to work, Shea!"

She sat down heavily on the corner of the table. "I don't believe this," she said. "You're being far too scrupulous."

Her bare thigh was only inches from his hand. "Maybe. But that's the way it is."

"I could make you change your mind."

An edge of steel to his voice, he said, "Don't even try."

"So it's because you can't paint..." She hesitated, marshaling her thoughts. Glancing over at the scattered bundles of paper on the table and the hearth, she said, "I'll give you back the sketch you did of me and you can paint that."

The unexpectedness of her offer, its sheer generosity, took Simon's breath away. "No," he said harshly.

She leaned forward. "Why not? If it's all right with me?"

To the best of his ability he tried to tell the truth. "It would be taking something intensely private that's only between you and me, and putting it on public display. Your body...it's mine, dammit, not anyone else's! I don't want the rest of the world seeing it." He ran his fingers through his hair. "It's not logical, it doesn't make sense—but that's the way it is."

"How can you say my body's yours when we haven't even made love?"

"I said it wasn't logical." Scowling, he grabbed one of the crutches and hitched himself up, going over to the sink to get a drink of water.

"Then surely you can find someone else to paint."

He drained the glass, the muscles in his throat working as he swallowed. Then, staring out of the window at the peaceful brown waters of the lake, he voiced his worst fear. "I'm afraid that I've lost myself—my essence—in the last five years. That I've sold my soul. Perhaps I'll never be able to paint again."

Swiftly Shea stationed herself in front of him, grasping him by the wrist. "I don't believe that!" she cried. "Maybe you're in a rut, or you've painted yourself into a corner. But you'll get out, Simon, I know you will."

Her eyes were afire with the sincerity of her belief. Unable to help himself, Simon pulled her into his arms, kissing her with a desperate hunger that had none of the tenderness of the night. She matched him kiss for kiss, holding nothing of herself back with the reckless courage that he loved. Against her mouth he whispered hoarsely, "My wild, beautiful Shea."

She pushed against him, saying shakily, "Promise me something. Promise you won't push me away again the way you did this morning. I hated it, Simon. You were playing games with me and it hurt."

He could lose himself in the gray mists of her irises, where pleading and the memory of pain were mingled. "I did what I thought was best."

Her arms tightened around his waist. "This is what's best," she said with utter conviction.

"I won't have an affair with you, Shea, until I've got my life sorted out!"

She stepped back from him, planting her hands on her hips. "You're missing the point altogether. This is a summer affair—a thing of the moment. Not a lifelong commitment. So what difference does it make whether you can paint or not?"

The words were dragged from somewhere deep within Simon; and as he spoke them he recognized in a way he scarcely understood how profoundly he was committed to her. "It's not a summer affair for me, Shea. I'm not talking about some kind of casual fling. You might be—but I'm not."

"You're as unbendable as steel," she said furiously. "Maybe if we had an affair you'd be able to paint again."

"And maybe I wouldn't—I won't risk it, do you hear me?"

"Then what are we going to *do*?"

"Try not to find ourselves alone like this," he said with a crooked smile that didn't reach his eyes. "Because I won't have any kind of relationship with you that's divorced from my feelings—I've been behaving that way for years."

She flung her words at him like a challenge. "I go back to work tomorrow. But I'm off on Tuesday."

"Jim'll be back by then."

Her eyes narrowed. "Compromise isn't a word in your vocabulary."

"Not on this one."

She crossed her arms over her chest. "I suppose I could take up mountain climbing. Or marathon running."

That she should want him as badly as he wanted her still seemed miraculous to Simon. "Cold showers are easier," he said.

"It's not funny! Two days ago I was saying I wouldn't have an affair with you. I change my mind and what happens? You've decided not to get involved with me." Glowering, she stalked over to the desk, still littered with crumpled paper. "May I look?"

He nodded, watching as she flattened sheet after sheet, her gaze intent. Then he saw her grimace, and stepped closer. It was the last sketch he had done of her. Shea in a rage, he could have called it, he thought, smiling at the accuracy with which he had captured her flared nostrils and tilted chin. In a sudden flash of insight he said, "My mother was Irish and my dad English, and they fought cat and dog all the years of their marriage. But I was never frightened even when I was young because I always knew they loved each other as passionately as they fought...sometimes you remind me of her."

"Two big differences," Shea said lightly. "I'm not married to you and I'm not in love."

Simon disliked quite thoroughly the promptness with which she had spoken. But before he could say anything Shea reared her head. "A car's coming down the driveway," she said, puzzled.

Simon had heard it at the same time as she. Doors slammed and footsteps ran up the outside steps. Then Jim walked in, holding the door open for a petite brunette with an enchanting smile. Jim strode over to his brother, punching him lightly on the chest, his eyes full of concern. "Are you okay, big brother?"

Simon grinned. "Nine hundred per cent better than yesterday."

"You don't look so hot."

Shea said warmly, "You didn't see him twenty-four hours ago."

Touched by his brother's evident concern, Simon said, "Thanks for coming back early, Jim. Now introduce me to your friend."

Jim's smile was both proprietorial and happy. "I persuaded Sally that she'd had enough of relatives for now and that I was wasting away without her." As Sally gave a rude snort, he added, "Well, metaphorically speaking. Anyway, I didn't think it was fair for Shea to have to take time off to look after you. Sally, this is my brother Simon. Simon, Sally Garrick. Hi there, Shea...you remember Sally."

Within a few minutes they were all sitting on the veranda drinking cold beer, eating nachos, and exchanging their news. Then Jim and Sally went for a swim to cool off after their long drive, while Shea and Simon started making a salad for supper. As Shea passed him the lettuce, Simon's hand brushed hers, and for a moment he stared at the pink ovals of her fingernails, recalling with graphic detail how they had tangled themselves in the hair on his chest in the middle of the night.

He glanced up. Shea said in a strangled voice, "When you look at me like that, I could just as easily put chocolate ice cream in the salad."

He put the lettuce on the counter and with one finger traced the delicate line of her cheekbone. "It's a good thing you go back to work tomorrow."

With characteristic directness she asked, "Will I see you on Tuesday?"

"Do you want to?"

She burst out, "There's a big part of me that says it's just fine that Simon won't have an affair with you, so back off, Shea, because you could get hurt no matter how careful you are. You've been hurt before, and it's no fun and you don't want that again." Ducking her head into the refrigerator, she brought out tomatoes and a rather limp bunch of celery. "The safe and sensible thing would be to call Phil or Larry and go to a movie in the city on Tuesday night."

The wrench in his guts was unquestionably jealousy. Turning the tap on to wash the romaine, Simon said shrewdly, "You'd be bored to tears."

She gave him a look of wide-eyed innocence. "You hope?"

He lowered his head and kissed her with imprudent thoroughness. "I know," he said.

"They're very nice men," she said, ignoring her heightened breathing with an aplomb he had to admire.

"Exactly."

"Not like you."

He shook out the lettuce in the sink. "Do I bore you?"

"No," she said gently. "But then neither do great white sharks."

He laughed out loud just as Jim came in the door, his wet hair curling around his ears. "What's the joke?" Jim asked.

"I think I've just been compared to a carnivore," Simon said amicably. "Want another beer?"

There was a lot of laughter around the supper table, and at a little after ten Shea got up to leave. Jim said placidly, "When did you say you're off—Tuesday? Why don't you come for dinner, Shea? Unless you've got other plans."

For a moment Shea looked as uncertain as a young girl. "I—all right," she said, avoiding Simon's eyes.

"Will you be okay in the canoe?" Simon said abruptly.

"There's a full moon, I'll be fine."

All too easily he could fantasize going back to her cabin and making love with her in the moonlight. She was right. He was a fool to let his scruples stand in the way of a love affair, he thought stormily, as Shea said good night and hurried out of the door. Tuesday seemed an age away.

The next few days sorely tried Simon's patience. Although Jim and Sally were very discreet, they were also in love. They touched each other a lot, and exchanged small, private glances, and he was certain that behind the closed bedroom door they made love every night. He missed Shea acutely.

In contrast to his inner turmoil, Simon's leg was healing remarkably quickly. With dogged persistence he sketched whenever he had privacy: much as he cared for his brother and liked Sally, he didn't want them watching every stroke of his pencil. He had tea and butterscotch squares with Minnie one afternoon, admired her garden and patted Tigger; and all the while he was wishing away the hours until he saw Shea again.

At five o'clock on Tuesday he went for a swim, partly to give Jim and Sally some time alone, but also because he needed to work off some of the tension that had been building in his body all day. He was an expert swimmer, and the cool slide and splash of the water was refreshing. He had swum into a cove the other side of the lake when he saw a canoe coming toward him. Shea was kneeling amidship, the gunwale nearly touching the water. Smoothly he began stroking toward her.

When he was only ten feet from the canoe, he stopped. Shaking back his wet hair, he said, "Want to go for a swim?"

She rested her paddle across her knees, the sunlight glinting in her hair. "Later," she said.

"Why not now? Jim and Sally are probably necking in the kitchen. We wouldn't want to disturb them."

She laughed unsympathetically. "Been a long week, hmm?"

"Excruciating." He took hold of the gunwale, smiling up at her. "What did you do all week?"

"Flew politicians around the countryside. Not what you'd call exciting. Your leg must be better."

"Yep. Did you phone Larry and Phil?"

"I did not."

He rocked the gunwale back and forth. "They wouldn't tip you in the lake. They're too nice."

"I'm wearing my best skirt and blouse," she said sternly.

"Take them off," he suggested. "No one's around."

"You are."

The skirt was flounced, tucked above her knees in the canoe, and the blouse softly outlined her breasts. Her gray eyes were laughing at him. "I missed you," he said.

She shifted her weight to balance herself better. "I thought about you quite a lot, too," she said, adding with a toss of her head, "If I take them off, will you make love to me?"

"In the lake?" he queried. "That might challenge my ingenuity."

"In my cabin. When you drive me home tonight."

His knuckles tightened on the wooden gunwale. "No, Shea."

"Perhaps I can change your mind," she said provocatively, tugging at the waistband of her skirt.

There were limits to his self-control, Simon thought, castigating himself for starting this. She pulled her blouse over her head, laid it carefully across the thwart, then stood up to take off her skirt. As the canoe swayed on the water, she gave a breathless laugh, and placed her skirt on top of her blouse. She was wearing flimsy and minimal lace underwear that revealed as much as they hid, and again Simon wondered if he was a fool not to make love to her. He was aware that, lighthearted though this scene might appear, a battle of wills was being fought on the lake. Shea thought making love would free his creativity, and he did not. Shea was convinced she could have an affair with him without any emotional entanglements, a premise he did not care for at all. So who was right? And who, he wondered, watching her nimbly hop from the canoe into the water and ducking from the splash, would win?

She surfaced, her hair streaming behind her head in long strands that reminded him inevitably of the very first time he had seen her. He had desired her then; he desired her now. She said, batting her wet lashes, "Your eyes are the same blue as the sky, Simon."

All right, he thought, you asked for it. He pulled her closer, unclasping her bra under the water and taking her breasts in his hands, all the while watching her eyes darken with passion. She said huskily, "That bra was expensive...if you lose it I'll make you dive to the bottom of the lake to get it."

He pulled it off, not without difficulty, and tossed it into the canoe. Then he submerged, caressing the wavering curves of her body in the cool water, burying his face in her navel, and only surfacing when he was gasping for air. They kissed, a long, lingering kiss during which they forgot to tread water and sank, sputtering, beneath the surface. They dived, playing with each other under the water, perhaps made bolder by the eerie silence of that other world, where her breasts were a pale shimmer, her legs pliant as the stems of the lilies, and her hair swayed about her head like grass in the wind.

This time they surfaced behind the canoe, which was slowly drifting across the cove. Simon touched her between her thighs, watching her face change, wanting to strip the last thin barrier of clothing from her body, haul her up on the land and possess her. He said, "We're playing with fire, Shea."

She managed a shaky laugh. "The water doesn't seem to be putting it out."

"Not what they taught us at fire-fighting school."

She wrinkled her wet nose endearingly. "Do you know one of the things I like about you, Simon?" she said. "Although maybe I shouldn't be saying this...Tim and I were very young, so sex was pretty rushed and unsubtle. But with Nicholas it was always rather solemn. We would Make Love. And it was somehow separate from the rest of our time together. He hated me to kiss him in public, he didn't even like holding hands on the street. So I love the way you and I laugh so much together." She hesitated, looking uncharacteristically flustered. "I hope you don't mind me saying that."

Another cord binding him to her looped itself around him. "I don't mind," he said.

"I like you," she said spontaneously.

Her guileless gray eyes, the sun glittering on the water, the clear blue of the sky all coalesced for Simon into a moment of perfect happiness. Happiness and a kind of security he had not experienced since the day his parents had died. If Shea said she would be there for you, he thought slowly, she would be there. No ifs or buts. Simply there.

A new kind of excitement stirred inside him. Was that what love was all about, he wondered, a strange and unsettling combination of ardor and comfort? They were not words he would have bracketed before. Certainly whatever he was feeling was new to him, and never before experienced, and for that he was glad. Whatever was between him and Shea, he wanted it to be unique.

She said quizzically, "You've gone a long way away."

"I'm happy," Simon replied, knowing instinctively that now was not the time to tell her all that he had been thinking.

"Oh." Briefly she looked disconcerted. With a finning motion of her hands she moved away from him in the water. "We should head for Jim's. He'll be wondering what's happened to us."

"Jim has other things on his mind," Simon said. "Are you happy, Shea? Right now, here with me?"

"Of course," she muttered. "Why wouldn't I be?"

The perfect moment was gone, ephemeral as a reflection on the water, and he was left with a strange sense of unease. "I suppose we should go back," he said.

In a clean overarm crawl Shea swam toward the canoe, and pulled herself over the gunwales in a move that bespoke both strength and practice. It also involved dragging her thighs across the hard wood. "I'll swim back," Simon called, watching the twist of her back as she dried herself on a towel and put on her blouse.

His leg was aching. He felt deeply uncertain of the woman who was even now paddling away from him across the lake. And that, too, was new to him.

CHAPTER SEVEN

AT NINE-fifteen Jim's telephone rang. The four of them were sitting in the living room, replete from barbecued chicken and rhubarb pie. Jim groaned and got to his feet. "Hello?" he said. Then his face sobered. "Yes, she's here...just a moment." Holding out the receiver, he said, "Shea, it's for you. It's Minnie's next-door neighbor."

Shea took the phone and held a brief, cryptic conversation. Putting it down, she said quietly, "Tigger—Minnie's dog—has been killed by a car. She's asking for me...can I borrow your car, Jim?"

"Sure. Poor old Minnie, she thought the world of that dog. Do you want company, Shea?"

"I think I'd better go on my own. I'll give you a call when I know what's going on." She gave Simon a quick, troubled smile and hurried out of the door. An hour later she phoned to say she would stay at Minnie's for the night if Jim didn't need the car.

The news had cast a damper on the evening. Jim and Sally went to bed shortly afterward, and Simon read far into the night. He was the only one up in the morning when the phone rang again. When he picked it up and said hello, Shea said, "Simon? If I came and got you, would you mind coming to Minnie's? She has a favor to ask of you."

"Of course I'll come. What does she want?"

"I have no idea. But she really does want to see you...I'll be there in fifteen minutes."

Minnie must be lost without the bouncy little mongrel who had gone everywhere with her, Simon thought soberly. He'd be glad to do anything she asked.

He found a clean shirt, changed the dressing on his leg, and was ready when Shea drove down the driveway. He went out on the veranda to meet her. The sky was overcast; he was wearing cotton pants and a blue shirt, his sleeves rolled up. Shea, of course, was wearing the same skirt and blouse. As she climbed the steps, she gave him a tired smile.

Without even thinking Simon took her in his arms, pressing her cheek into his shoulder. Against his chest she said, "Minnie thinks she didn't latch the gate properly last night and that's how Tigger got out. So she's feeling guilty on top of sad. I feel so sorry for her."

Simon held her close, saying eventually, "We'll go to your cabin so you can change and get your car... have you eaten?"

She nodded. "I wanted Minnie to eat something, so I cooked breakfast. I sure would like to get out these clothes, though. I slept in them."

Simon left a note for Jim, and a few minutes later was surveying the interior of Shea's cabin while she showered. It was cool and uncluttered, the wicker furniture covered with an inexpensive but attractive floral print, the books neatly arranged on the shelves. His sketch was pinned to the wall by the window that overlooked the lake.

When Shea came back into the room, she was wearing white culottes with an embroidered sweater in frosted pink, her hair in a damp cloud around her face. "I feel like a human being again," she said. "Shall we go?"

Her lipstick matched her sweater. She looked as cool and uncluttered as her room; she also looked untouchable. Which was, Simon thought grimly, very conscious of her bedroom to his right, probably wise.

He drove to Jim's in his brother's car, left it there, and continued into the village with Shea. The gate to Minnie's was firmly latched, and the garden was a riot of glowing color under the gray sky. Simon followed Shea into the trailer. Minnie was sitting at the table. Although her eyes were reddened from weeping, she was composed, and accepted Simon's condolences with a dignity that sat well on her small figure. Shea poured three cups of coffee from the percolator on the stove, and Minnie plunged into her request. "I hadn't had Tigger very long," she said, her fingers playing with her apron. "Only two years. So I don't have any photos of him to remember him by." For a moment her voice broke. She blew her nose, and, looking Simon straight in the eye, went on, "You're an artist and you saw Tigger two or three times. You could paint me a picture of him, couldn't you?"

There was an instant of dead silence. Simon sneaked a look at Shea, who was looking as flabbergasted as no doubt he was; whatever he had expected, it had not been this. Minnie said hastily, "I know you're very famous, and perhaps I shouldn't be asking you—but there wasn't anyone else." She paused. "Maybe you don't remember what he looked like, though."

One of Simon's gifts was an almost photographic memory. "I remember," he said slowly.

"I'd pay you, of course," Minnie said.

A single portrait of Simon's could buy her entire trailer and all its contents. Simon said, "I'm only hesitating because you took me by surprise. And there'll be no question of payment, Minnie."

"You mean you'll do it?" she said, her voice rising hopefully.

Clearly she had been afraid that he would refuse. "Of course I will," Simon said, and heard his own words echo in his head.

Tears filled her eyes. She blinked them back and quavered, "Thank you, Simon."

He smiled at her, knowing he could not possibly have refused. "There will be payment," he said. "A butterscotch square every time I come to visit you."

"Not only that—I'll make a whole box for you to take home with you to England," she promised.

Home to England . . . he no longer knew where home was, he thought in confusion, avoiding Shea's eyes. "It may take me a while," he said.

"You take as long as you want," Minnie said comfortably. "It's very kind of you . . . I feel better already knowing I'll have a picture of Tigger."

They finished their coffee, a neighbor dropped in to bring Minnie's lunch, and Shea and Simon left, Shea having promised to stay the night again. The gate shut with a click behind them. "Well," said Simon, "now I have to paint, don't I?"

"Have you got any supplies?" Shea asked pragmatically.

He hadn't even thought of supplies. "Not as much as a brush. I'd better head for Halifax and buy some . . . why don't you come with me, Shea? I'll take you out for dinner afterward."

"A date," she said suspiciously.

"That's right. You'll be quite safe because you're staying the night with Minnie."

She looked at him through her lashes. "You probably shouldn't drive with your sore leg."

"Absolutely not."

"All right," she said.

They went back to Jim's cabin to tell him what they were doing and for Simon to get his wallet. Then they set off for the city. By unspoken agreement they kept the conversation on impersonal matters—books they had read and movies they had seen, getting to know each other's likes and dislikes. Shea parked the car on a side street and they walked to the art store, the breeze from the ocean blowing her hair back.

In a comprehensive survey Simon saw that the shop was more than adequate. Not giving himself time to think, he went to the rack of brushes, swiftly picking out several, then adding solvent, some tubes of paint, and a palette. There were two large stacks of ready-made canvases against the wall. And here he stopped dead, as though he were physically paralyzed. The canvases were very white and utterly blank. Swamped by a thousand memories of the hours he had spent in his studio last winter mocked by similar stretches of empty white canvas, he felt panic tighten his throat.

He had promised Minnie. He had committed himself to paint, of all things, the portrait of a mongrel dog. But what if he couldn't?

He would lose Minnie's respect. He would also lose any chance of a relationship with Shea.

As if his thoughts had conjured her up, Shea said quietly, "What's wrong, Simon?"

As he turned to face her, he saw her eyes widen with shock. God knew what he looked like, he thought savagely. "Portrait of the artist unable to paint," he rasped. "Do you know what I hate most about this, Shea? It's such a cliché, all this tormented artist stuff... and here I am, living it."

"Clichés are clichés because they speak a truth," she said. "What size canvas do you want?"

Trying to slow the rapid beat of his heart in his rib cage, he picked out several, along with some pure linen canvas and wooden stretcher bars. They carried his purchases to the cash register. Simon paid for them, the girl wrapped them, and he and Shea walked out into the street again. "We'll lock this stuff in the trunk of my car," Shea suggested. "Then we could buy some fish and chips and eat lunch down by the waterfront."

Simon could think of nothing to say. Fifteen minutes later they were sitting on a bench that overlooked the harbor, unwrapping paper packages they had bought at a stand. Sprinkling his fish with vinegar, Simon began to eat. The fish was fresh and the chips crisp; he tried to concentrate on the food and block out everything else.

Shea said hesitantly, "Can you tell me how this has happened—that you can't paint, I mean?"

She was licking grease from her fingers. He said, "I haven't talked to anyone about it. In London it would have been all over the city in no time."

"I won't tell anyone."

He could trust her, he was sure of that. Slowly at first, then losing himself in the story, he started with his childhood, the death of his parents, and his years of skirting the edge of the law. "That all changed when I got into art school. I was working too hard to have the time to get into trouble. I was ferociously ambitious. I took elocution lessons because my accent wouldn't do, I learned the basic social graces and the art of conversation—I remade myself from a kid from the docks to a man-about-town whom the critics were starting to notice." Gazing at the ferry approaching the dock, he went on, "I subdued everything to that ambition—to get to the top. Although I was dirt-poor for years, I made sure I had a good address, and on the few times I did go out I went where I would be seen and I took the right kind of woman. My sex life, my emotional life, everything was swallowed up in a drive to become one of the best portrait painters in the country.''

As he fell silent, Shea prompted, ''What happened when you did?''

''For a few years it was wonderful. I made a lot of money and spent a lot, I learned how to sail in the Bahamas and ski in the Alps, and I painted some portraits that I still think are good. And then, so gradually that I didn't realize what was happening until it was too late, it all went sour. Nothing that I painted had soul in it...no essence, no life. Only one of the critics picked up on it, although as soon as he did I knew he was right. And then I found I couldn't paint at all.''

A sea gull swooped past in a graceful arc. ''Maybe you were painting the wrong people,'' Shea said.

''I'd lost the stimulation, the inner spark from which any of my best portraits grew,'' Simon said with painful exactitude. ''Perhaps I remade myself so thoroughly that I lost myself in the process.''

''But since you've come here, you might be reversing that process—going back to your roots,'' she said with growing excitement. ''You and Jim seem to be getting closer all the time, and fire fighting is more like being a kid from the docks than painting portraits would be.''

It was a novel point of view. ''But you're leaving out the most important person—yourself,'' he said, and even as he spoke he recognized that his feelings for Shea were as fierce and all-encompassing as those between his parents had been. So in his reach for the top had he also smothered his emotional heritage?

"You were so beautiful in the lake yesterday," he said. She flushed, stabbing at a chip with her plastic fork. "Shea, is the only reason you want to make love to me because you think that's the key to my starting to paint again?"

The color in her cheeks deepened. Her lashes hiding her eyes, she said, "Well, there is that, yes. But I'd want to anyway. Look how we behave when we get within ten feet of each other, Simon! That's never happened to me before."

"So that's all? It's a case of practicality coupled with body chemistry?"

"Do you have to analyze everything?"

"Where you're concerned, yes. There's no other reason?"

She looked him full in the eye. "What else could there be?"

"What else indeed?" he said slowly, and was aware again of that spreading unease. He was quite sure that more than chemistry was pulling him to Shea. But he didn't know whether he should call it love...

By seven that evening Simon and Shea were driving back to Somerville. They had gone to a movie in the afternoon and eaten wonderfully spicy curry in an Indian restaurant afterward. They had not reopened the discussion on sexual attraction.

As they approached the outskirts of the village Shea said, "I leave for Yarmouth tomorrow—a fire a few miles inland. I'll be gone at least six days."

Something that had been nagging at Simon was suddenly clear. "Would you do me a favor?" he asked. "Would you let me use your cabin as a studio while you're gone? I didn't know how I was going to manage with Jim and Sally around all the time."

"I—I guess so...the cabin's my hideaway, Simon, it's a big part of my life. I didn't even invite Nicholas there very often."

"I'm different from Nicholas," he said forcefully.

She geared down at the approach of the village. "You can say that again," she said. "Yes, you can have the cabin. We'll go there now and I'll give you the extra key. In fact, if you want to drive me to the depot early tomorrow morning—and I mean early—you can have my car."

She had been honest about her doubts, and had then responded with far more than he had asked. "There's not a mean bone in your body...thanks."

"My contribution to Tigger's portrait," she said fliply, and turned down the dirt road to her cabin.

Simon pulled her canoe up on the dock while she packed, and within half an hour they were drawing up outside Minnie's. There was no one in sight. Simon leaned over and kissed Shea, taking his time and plainly enjoying himself. Then he smiled at her. "I'll see you at five-thirty—that way I'll find out what you're like first thing in the morning."

"It's just chemistry!" she said violently.

"I'm not Tim and I'm not Nicholas, will you get that through your thick head?" Simon replied in sudden irritation. "And we aren't going to start a fight outside Minnie's trailer."

She gave him a dirty look, scrambled out of the car, and grabbed her bag from the back seat. "Good night," she snapped, and marched toward the gate. Simon drove off.

*   *   *

When Simon arrived back at five twenty-five the next morning, Shea was walking down Minnie's path, the knees of her flying suit brushed by scarlet salvia and flimsy-petaled poppies. Her hair was in a businesslike braid. She gave him a guarded smile and climbed in the car.

"I won't eat you," Simon said, pulling away from the kerb. "Did you sleep well?"

"I kept dreaming about you," she muttered.

He laughed out loud. "If I were to paint one particular dream of you that I had last night, I'd be arrested on an obscenity charge. Would you visit me in jail, darling Shea?"

"I'd already be in the next cell," she said darkly. Then she tugged at her flight bag. "I brought some coffee in my thermos—want some?"

"You're a jewel among women," Simon said fervently. "That's almost enough to make me propose to you."

She gave him a demure smile. "Minnie sent some blueberry muffins so you could propose to her, too."

"Bigamy is a more serious offense than obscenity—I'll stick to one woman at a time."

"Do you joke about everything?" she demanded.

"You bolt like a frightened pony if I get serious about anything except sex."

"An affair doesn't have to be a love affair," she cried.

"Would it be so awful if you fell in love with me?"

"I don't want to! The two times I fell in love, I got hurt."

"Yet you say you want a husband and children as well as your job. This mythical husband—is it going to be a nice aseptic relationship with no messy emotions?"

"Simon, I have to fly to Yarmouth in half an hour," she said tightly. "This is no time for an argument ... the depot's up the next road to the right."

Simon took a bite of muffin and put on his indicator. "Think about it," he said. Shea said nothing.

Five minutes later he drew up by the hangar; the blue helicopter was parked on the cement pad outside. He said evenly, "Take care of yourself, Shea."

"I'll call when I'm ready to fly home, if you want to pick me up here?" Simon nodded. "Good luck with Tigger," she added, her eyes very serious. Impulsively she leaned over and brushed his lips with hers. Then she got out of the car. As she disappeared through the side door of the hangar, she gave him a quick wave.

He wouldn't see her for at least six days. Six days isn't forever, Simon told himself stringently. Besides, you've got work to do.

And Simon did work, with an intensity that made him as tired in its own way as fire fighting had. His commitment to Minnie got him over the hurdle of actually putting his brush to canvas, and at the end of three days he had completed two small oils. The next day he lined them up in the early morning light on Shea's kitchen counter and looked at them, frowning. He had caught Tigger's bumptious energy rather well, he thought critically. Minnie would no doubt be delighted with either one of them. More than delighted.

But he wasn't. He wanted more. He wanted to give Minnie the very best he was capable of.

Not for the sake of his reputation. Certainly not for money. Rather because his integrity was at stake.

Restlessly he prowled around Shea's living room. She wouldn't be back for two more days, he thought, wishing that she were here now, aching to hold her in his arms. He remembered her coming down Minnie's path in the soft dawn light on the last morning he had seen her, the crinkled heads of the poppies swaying as she walked past them—and suddenly stood still, his heart beginning to thud in his chest. Tempera, not oils, he thought. I've been using the wrong medium. A large panel in egg tempera of the garden... that's where I've got to start.

He tried blocking out a composition in his sketchpad. He drove to Minnie's and studied the garden through narrowed eyes, making several drawings and attracting an audience of two small boys armed with fishing rods; he then had tea with Minnie, his pencil flying over the paper as she talked about Tigger. He spent the rest of the day producing sketch after sketch, tearing most of them up but keeping a few. By evening the composition was starting to take a shape that pleased him.

Early the next day he drove to Halifax in Shea's car to buy more supplies; in the pale morning light he was attacked by fears that he was merely delaying the inevitable disappointment that had dogged his work for over a year now. Did he really think a change of medium would solve all his problems?

Trying to subdue doubts which, he knew, could immobilize him if he allowed them to, he bought pigments and a gesso panel at the art store, and farm-fresh eggs at the market. Back at Shea's he mixed the pigments with water and transferred his drawing to the panel. At first light the following day he started to paint.

When the phone rang that afternoon he was hard at work. It was a man's voice, not Shea's. "Michael Dalton here, Simon—the pilot you met at the base camp. Shea won't get in until tomorrow morning so she asked me to call you. If you wanted to be at the depot around eleven, she'd be ready to go by then.''

Conscious of a keen disappointment that he wouldn't see her tonight, Simon hung up, cleaned his brushes, and went to see Jim. Sally had gone shopping in the city with a girlfriend; he and Jim went for a swim, then sat on the veranda drinking beer. ''You've put in quite a week,'' Jim observed. ''I always thought artists dashed off masterpieces in fits of inspiration and spent the rest of their time making love and drinking red wine.''

Simon hoisted his beer can. ''The Nova Scotian equivalent?'' he said lazily.

''Shea's pretty wary of you.''

''We are not spending our time making love,'' Simon announced.

''For all her brave talk about combining job, marriage and kids, I'm not so sure she's convinced it'll ever happen,'' Jim said reflectively. ''That Nicholas was a smooth-tongued bastard if ever there was one. He pulled the rug right out from under her. For that matter, I thought he was on the up-and-up as well. So it's no wonder she's scared.''

''The way I feel around her is the way Dad felt about Mom,'' Simon said. ''Theirs wasn't what you'd call a reasonable relationship.''

Jim leaned forward. ''Tell me about them, Simon. I don't remember them at all.''

So for nearly two hours Simon talked about his parents and his upbringing, sharing memories with the man to whom they would mean the most, and, he knew, further cementing the bond between him and his brother. When they heard Sally turning into the driveway, Jim laid a hand on Simon's arm. ''Thanks,'' he said huskily, and Simon saw that there were tears in his eyes.

"Any time," he said gently. "I haven't told you the story about Mom and the rent collector yet. We'll save that for another day."

Sally was bubbling over with the pleasure of her purchases, and the mood changed. But before Jim and Sally went to bed that night Jim gave his brother a clumsy hug; Simon slept like a log. When he went over to Shea's the next morning to paint, he was well content. By traveling to this country he had gained a brother and regained his ability to work. And today he would see Shea again.

CHAPTER EIGHT

ALTHOUGH Simon arrived at the depot early, not wanting to miss Shea, the blue helicopter was not parked on the pad. After searching the sky for it, he went into the hangar. A gray-haired man sitting in an office waved him in. "Bill Dugan," he said, shaking hands. "You come for Shea?"

"Simon Greywood. Yes, I was to meet her here."

"There'll be a delay—I tried to phone you, but you'd already left. A bird collided with the tail rotor so she's down in the middle of a bog. Trouble is——"

"*Down*?" Simon repeated blankly, a cold fist clenching in his belly.

"It's okay," Bill said hastily, "no need to worry. I forgot you wouldn't know the lingo. She's fine—she made a perfect landing." As Simon sat down heavily in the nearest chair, Bill went on pedantically, "When the tail rotor's damaged, you've got to land as soon as you can—you lose all your stability. She brought the machine down in a bog about thirty miles inland. No roads within easy reach, so she'll have to stay there until our other 'copter gets back. Around three, that should be. Then we'll go get her. She knows what's up. You don't have a worry in the world."

He must have looked awful for Bill to be ladling out reassurances so liberally, Simon thought. "If I get back here at two-thirty, can I go along for the ride?" he asked.

"Sure thing. You do that. If the time changes, I'll let you know."

126

So at two-thirty Simon again pulled up in the depot parking lot. Michael was standing near a maroon helicopter that was being refueled. He waved at Simon. "We'll be ready in about ten minutes," he called.

They lifted off shortly afterward. Simon enjoyed the flight, knowing Shea would be at the end of it. Michael was happy to have company, pointing out two moose in the middle of a swamp, the charred patch of a small burn near some cottages, and some local landmarks. As always, the sheer expanse of the forest amazed Simon, used as he was to the neatly apportioned English countryside.

Michael, it transpired, had become engaged only two weeks ago. Simon listened to a lengthy description of how he and Catherine had met, and into a pause said curiously, "Did you never date Shea?"

Michael laughed. "Nope. I really like Shea, she's a gorgeous gal and a great pilot, and I'd trust her with my life—but I guess I'm the old-fashioned kind. When I get home after a hard day's work, I want my wife there at the door and the dinner cooked. Shea would just as likely be off flying somewhere herself." He peered downwards. "I'd better check her coordinates. We should be getting close."

So Shea was entirely accurate to realize that what she offered was not everyone's cup of tea; Michael's name could be added to the list of Tim, Nicholas and Peter. Whereas Simon had always thought that a conventional marriage had a high potential for being deadly dull. Smiling to himself, he scanned the ground. They were flying over an area of scrub brush and marsh, dotted with lakes that merged with taller trees. Then as Michael brought his machine around in a wide arc Simon saw the blue helicopter parked in solitary state on a patch of marsh grass. Michael gave a grunt of satisfaction. "We can land right beside it...let's hope there aren't any more birds around."

The ground rushed up to meet them, the grass and the small tamaracks bowing to the down draught. The helicopter touched down with the lightest of bumps and Michael throttled back, waiting for the oil temperature to cool. Shea's helicopter was on Simon's side of the cockpit. She was not sitting inside it, waiting for them. She was not standing on the grass, waving at them. She wasn't anywhere in sight.

With growing anxiety Simon craned his neck to search the surroundings. There were no trees tall enough to hide her from view. He said into the intercom, "I can't see her, Michael."

"She's probably on the other side of her 'copter, keeping out of the wind. Surprised she wasn't sitting inside—the flies are bad at this time of year."

As Michael closed the throttle and cut off the fuel, the rotor blades began to slow. "Keep low, Simon, and stay away from the exhaust. I'll take a look at the damage before we leave and we'll send a repair crew out tomorrow."

Simon climbed out, ducking until he was beyond reach of the blades, his clothes flattened to his body. "Shea!" he yelled.

The red-banded tail rotor on Shea's helicopter was bent out of shape, a small patch of feathers adhering to it. When Simon walked around it, Shea was nowhere in sight. Maybe she fell asleep waiting for us, he thought, and shouted her name, louder this time. His heart pounding with the thick strokes of fear, he opened the door of her machine and swiftly discovered it was empty. There were sandwich wrappers crumpled on the seat beside hers. He stared at them, mesmerized, wishing they could speak.

A crow cawed in the distance, and the swish of Michael's rotors gradually diminished. As Simon closed the door of Shea's helicopter, a mosquito whined in his ear, and then another...she couldn't have lain down outside, she'd have been eaten alive. "Shea!" he shouted again.

Michael joined him. "No sign of her?"

"None. Where the devil can she be?"

"She didn't leave a note?"

They did a quick survey of the cockpit, finding nothing out of place but a package of chewing gum under her seat. "I can't figure this out," Michael said, a frown furrowing his forehead. "She must have gone for a walk to pass the time—maybe she got lost."

Into Simon's mind dropped an image of the miles of wilderness they had flown over. If Shea got lost in that, they might never find her. "We'd better get help," he said sharply.

"She could have fallen asleep under a tree," Michael said soothingly. "She wouldn't thank us for alerting the search and rescue people if that's the case. We'll do an aerial survey first, check out the surroundings."

For over thirty minutes they flew in low circles over the marshes and woods around Shea's helicopter, until Simon's eyes ached with the strain of trying to pick out the beige of her flight suit among the shrubs and trees. Then Michael touched down again. "I'll contact the base and see what they advise—why don't you look around for footprints?"

For a few moments Simon stood at the nose of Shea's helicopter, trying to put himself in her shoes, wondering what she might have done. It was very hot, although not as hot as it would have been at high noon. The mosquitoes and blackflies would have fastened on her voraciously almost as soon as she left the helicopter; but she'd known she had a delay of at least five hours before the other helicopter would arrive.

To his right he saw the gleam of a lake past the tangled shrubs of bayberry and lambkill, and when he brought his gaze lower he saw the bruised and broken stems of grass where someone had walked. His pulse racing in his ears, he began to trace the footsteps, and now that he was attuned to them he could see that they were heading for the lake. Shea, whom he had first seen delighting in the water, had gone for a swim.

Then why wasn't she back?

Ice-cold fingers clamped around his heart. She couldn't have drowned. Not Shea, his beautiful, vibrant Shea who was as at home in the water as an otter.

As though it were from another planet, he heard Michael's voice calling his name. He turned back, quickly described what he had found, and said he was going to follow the footsteps as best he could. "We can't get another machine in for at least three hours," Michael reported. "We'd best pack some emergency first aid and go after her ourselves. I'll radio the depot and let them know what we're doing. The fly dope's in the first-aid kit, Simon. And there are boots in the survival gear."

They set off five minutes later, Simon leading the way. Trying to ignore the cold knot of fear lodged like a stone in his gut, he walked as fast as he could, his boots squelching in the wet ground, his eyes searching for the signs of Shea's progress. Although the heat made him sweat and the swarms of blackflies were a constant irritant, he was largely oblivious to both. Shea . . . he had to find Shea.

The grass was soon swallowed up by thickets of leather-leafed shrubs. Simon stopped, looking for broken branches. "Maybe we should head right for the lake," he said. "I'd swear that's where she was going."

They ploughed through the undergrowth, emerging ten minutes later on the shores of a small lake. Simon could see no sign that Shea had swum there. The wind had dropped, and the water was the same dark color of the lake at Jim's; it's polished surface mocked him with its impenetrability.

"Quit worrying," Michael said incisively. "Shea might not be everyone's idea of the perfect housekeeper, but she's not dumb, either, and she's one of the best swimmers I know. I don't have a clue where she is, but I'm sure she's safe."

Simon looked blankly at the other man. I love Shea, he thought. I love her. That's why I'm standing here terrified out of my mind that something's happened to her.

Michael grabbed him by the sleeve, shaking his arm. "She wouldn't have swum there. It's too shallow and there are too many reeds. Come on, we'll go to the next lake."

With an actual physical effort Simon brought his attention back to what the other man was saying; and belatedly his brain started working again. Michael was right. Shea would have bypassed this lake for the larger one farther on, which on its far shore was flanked by the tall spires of spruce and fir trees. With a great leap of his pulse he saw a freshly broken clod of grass a few feet away, and beyond it a clump of bent reeds.

They covered the ground to the next lake in record time, Simon's acute vision picking up further traces where Shea had walked. The second lake was much larger; of one accord the two men headed for the small sand beach halfway along its length.

In the sand they found Shea's tracks—the indented soles of her sneakers and the imprint of her bare feet. There was no sign of her clothes. In a wave of relief that left him weak at the knees, Simon realized she had not drowned here in a lake where no one would have heard her cries. For Shea, he thought, would have swum naked.

He looked around, again trying to imagine what she might have done next. The swim would have refreshed her, and she still had two or three hours before she would be rescued. The forest would have beckoned, with its promise of coolness and its shelter from the hot rays of the sun. And if she was in the forest, they wouldn't have spotted her from the helicopter.

The ground was drier and he was unable to pick up any more footprints as he and Michael tramped toward the trees. When they got closer, Michael called a halt. "She could have gone up that slope or into the trees on the right there...I think we should separate, Simon." He pulled a couple of compasses out of his backpack. "You know how to use one of these?" Simon nodded. "Okay. We'll meet back here in two hours. If we haven't found her by then, I think we should bring in the police. Which way do you want to go?"

The stream that fed into the lake disappeared into the forest on Simon's right, and through the trees he could hear the chuckle of water over rocks. "I'll go to the right." Checking his watch, he added, "See you later," and with a pang remembered how Shea so often said "see you" instead of goodbye.

As Michael vanished among the trees, Simon set off along the stream. The forest floor was uneven with rotting stumps and boulders, and smelled damply of moss: a green sanctuary that could be reduced to smoking stumps and barren black soil with horrifying speed. The fields of Sussex had never engendered in him such protectiveness, he thought, striding up the hill through thigh-deep ferns. Shea had just spent a week battling a fire; surely this was the way she would have come.

Shea, whom he loved. He began calling her name at intervals, standing still to listen for any response. The tiny cheeps of foraging kinglets and the gurgle of the brook were all he could hear; that, and the heavy pounding of his own heart.

He had been climbing for perhaps half an hour when he saw moss newly scraped off a boulder by the edge of the stream. So she had come this way, he thought jubilantly, and shouted her name again.

A couple of minutes later he stopped in his tracks. The base of the tree straight ahead of him had been ripped open, earth scattered over the ground. Shea had not done that. That was the sort of thing bears did.

Black bears, especially females with cubs, had been known to attack humans. A new fear fueling his steps, Simon hauled himself up a steep granite embankment. Right in front of him was a tree trunk scored with long, deep scratches.

The hair rose on the back of his neck. "Shea!" he yelled, and saw that the stream had forked into two. Wouldn't she have turned back when she saw the bear signs?

Unless the bear had come through after her. Was pursuing her.

Going on intuition, he took the left-hand fork, his pace quickening, his eyes darting among the trees as though he were a hunter. He pushed his way through a small stand of spruce, snapping off some of the lower branches as he did so. It was a good idea, Jim had told him, to make as much noise as you could in bear country, for it was dangerous to take one by surprise.

Ahead of him a majestic pine with wide-spread limbs had carpeted the ground in soft, springy needles. At another time he might have wanted to sketch it. As it was, he stopped underneath it and shouted Shea's name.

From directly above him a small voice said, "Simon, is that you?"

For a moment Simon was sure he was dreaming, that the desperation of his search had conjured Shea up in his imagination. He looked up. "Shea?" he said hoarsely.

He heard scuffling, then a small shower of needles sifted down on his head. "I'm up here. I thought you were another bear."

"Are you all right?" he demanded, circling the pine until he finally saw her. She was wedged between two branches and the trunk; she was high enough that she looked very small.

Her voice already stronger, she said, "I'm cramped and thirsty and I've been eaten alive by mosquitoes. But I'm *very* glad to see you . . . you are really there, aren't you? I'm not dreaming you?"

Never in his entire life had he been so happy to see someone. "I'm here," he said. "Why didn't you answer when I shouted?"

"I kept falling asleep. Maybe that's what woke me up."

Nothing could have stopped the grin splitting his face. "How long have you been up there?"

With some difficulty she consulted her watch. "Two hours and eleven minutes. I saw a bear, that's the reason I'm up here."

"Are you coming down?"

"I'm stuck," she said succinctly. "I'm scared of heights."

By now thoroughly enjoying himself, Simon said, "A pilot who's scared of heights is worse than an artist who can't paint."

"I don't think that's very funny," she said with great dignity. "When I'm flying, there's a helicopter between me and the ground."

"So do I have to rescue you?"

"It would be nice."

Simon's teenage years had included aspirations to become a cat burglar. After assessing the tree with professional eyes, he swung himself up by one of the lowermost branches, hoping it would bear his weight. Then with strong, economical movements he climbed higher, until he was on a level with Shea. "Hello there," he said.

She gave him a tremulous smile. "I *am* glad to see you. I was afraid I might be here all night."

There were patches of dried blood on her neck where blackflies had bitten her, and her hair had bits of twig and bark in it. He said, "Darling Shea, I'm glad to see you, too. I had you crashed, drowned, and eaten alive by a bear, all since midday—I only hope you enjoyed your swim."

Her eyes glinted. "It was lovely. No stray artists watching me."

He wedged himself more comfortably in the crook of two big branches. "Tell me about the bear."

"I was wandering along enjoying the stream and the lovely ferns, and then I saw this tree and thought how beautiful it was...why are you smiling?"

"Because that's exactly what I thought you'd be doing. Go on."

"So I sat down underneath it, and the next thing you know I'd dozed off. The sounds of the bear woke me. It must have been scratching a tree or something. I was terrified. I got partway up the tree in record time, and when I saw it come over the rise I climbed higher. It wandered around the clearing for a while then disappeared—I don't think it was the slightest bit interested in me. But by then I knew I couldn't get down. End of story."

Simon unclasped his water jug from his belt and passed it to her. She took a long drink, splashed a bit on her hands and face, then gave it back. "Now what?" she said.

"I'll go down the tree ahead of you—you'll be between me and the trunk, so you'll be quite safe," Simon said. "Try not to look at the ground."

"I wouldn't think of it," Shea said, shuddering.

She was noticeably paler. Simon braced himself firmly, then helped her to stand, easing her around so that her back was toward him. "I'm going to put my foot on the next branch down, and then you'll do the same," he said calmly. "Your left foot, Shea."

He suited action to his words. Her body rigid with fear, she lowered her leg to the branch and shifted her weight. "That's right. Now your other leg," Simon said.

Branch by branch he coaxed her down. She didn't say a word, the tension in her slender body speaking for itself. When they were only twenty feet from the ground, her foot slipped on a piece of loose bark. She gasped with terror, grabbing for the trunk. Simon held her hard, one arm so tight under her breast that he could feel the frantic racing of her heart. "Shea, I won't let you fall," he said forcibly. "We're nearly there. A few more minutes and this'll be over."

He could hear her breathing in shallow gasps. He looked down, realizing that the last few feet would be the most difficult because the branches were more widely spaced. "Take hold of these two boughs," he said, guiding her hands to them. "I'm going to climb down to the next branch and then I'll lift you down, okay?"

She nodded, her wrists taut with strain. As Simon lifted her, it took all his strength to keep his own balance and hold her weight as well; he felt a twinge of pain in his left leg. Looking down, he planned the next move, got her on a lower branch, and said, "I'm going to jump to the ground now, then I'll catch you when you jump. Hold on until I tell you to let go."

The carpet of needles was soft enough to break his fall. He stood up and said, "You can jump now, Shea."

Blindly she obeyed him. She landed almost on top of him, knocking him sideways, their bodies rolling together on the forest floor. Lying on his side and clasping her to his chest, Simon realized she was trembling in reaction. He held her close, raining little kisses on her hair. "It's all right, sweetheart, it's over and you're safe."

She muttered something incomprehensible into his shirt. The warm curves of her body, so well remembered, and the softness of her hair against his cheek suddenly overwhelmed Simon with emotion. He said roughly, "I thought you were dead, or that we might never find you...I don't think I've ever been as frightened in my entire life. Shea, darling Shea, I love you so much."

Her body went still in his arms. Then she pushed against his chest. "Don't, Simon," she said in a choked voice. "Please don't say that!"

Ignoring her, he let the words spill out. "You must know I love you—I'm sure I'm the only one who was too slow to see what was going on. It took that first lake, where I thought you'd drowned, to make me realize how I feel about you...I was so afraid that it was too late."

"I don't want you to be in love with me," she cried frantically, sitting upright and tugging at her flying suit to straighten it. "You'll spoil everything."

"How can love spoil anything?" he demanded, getting to his feet and pulling her upright. "It can only enrich what's between us."

"You might love me but I don't love you," she said with suppressed violence. "And I don't want to. Oh, for heaven's sake, Simon, let's get out of here. I'm tired and hot and I want to be home in my own cabin."

Which was littered with all his art supplies. He said impetuously, "I thought you were dead—don't you understand? Did you expect me to waltz up to you and say oh, how nice to find you alive and well? Have a heart, Shea!"

"I'm sorry you had that experience and I'm truly grateful to you for getting me down that awful tree—but I'm not in love with you! *I'm* going back to the helicopter, Simon, and you can do what you want."

Angrier than he had ever been in all the time he had known her, Simon seized her by the elbow. "Be very careful what you're saying, Shea—because if you're too frightened to risk falling in love again I'm sure as hell not going to sleep with you. The reason I want you so badly is because I love you, and that means building something between us. Something that'll last. Something beautiful. But I can't do it alone and I won't beg for whatever crumbs you're willing to offer me as if I'm a starving goddammed dog.''

"I will not be made to feel guilty because I don't love you, Simon Greywood," she snapped, yanking her arm free, her breast heaving.

And finally her words penetrated. She means it, Simon thought numbly. She really doesn't love me. Worse, she doesn't want to love me. He reached for the nearest branch of the pine tree for support, feeling as though someone had just kicked him in the stomach.

"I can't stand this," Shea said wildly. She whirled, dodging through the spruce trees until she reached the granite embankment. Stooping, she slithered down it and out of sight.

Simon stayed where he was, knowing at some level of his mind that if she followed the stream she couldn't get lost. It hurt him to breathe. His knees felt as though he'd just completed a twenty-mile hike through a bog, and his left thigh ached. He let go of the branch, rubbing his palm down his bush pants, aware that if he looked down he would see that his hands were shaking.

He might have stood there for an hour if it hadn't occurred to him that Shea, in her headlong flight down the brook, might run into the bear. He climbed down the granite rock face and followed the water, oblivious to the softly shaded greens of the ferns and mosses. Absently he looked at his watch, astounded that so little time had passed; Michael wasn't due back at their rendezvous for another twenty minutes.

When he reached the edge of the trees, Shea was waiting for him. She gave his face a quick glance and looked away. "I wasn't sure which way to go."

The contours of the land hid the two helicopters from sight. "We have to wait for Michael," Simon said. "He went looking for you up that slope."

He passed her the fly dope. As she took the bottle from him, he noticed with a surge of bitterness how careful she was not to touch him. Sitting down on a rock, schooling his brain to emptiness, he waited for the other man. Six minutes later when Michael strode out of the trees, Shea ran to meet him. With a sense of utter detachment Simon watched them hug each other and walk back toward him. He got up, said with creditable normality, "You had a long walk for nothing, Michael," and set off through the undergrowth toward the nearer lake. Behind him he could hear Shea telling Michael about the bear. He hated her for being able to carry on such an ordinary conversation.

When they got back to the helicopter, he sat in the back. Michael flew to the depot, Shea filed a report, and then she came outside to where Simon was waiting in her car. As she got in the passenger seat he said, "I'll take my stuff out of your cabin tonight."

"How's the painting going?" she asked in a stilted voice.

"Fine."

With an ostentatious sigh of weariness Shea leaned back and closed her eyes. Simon drove to Somerville. When he turned into her driveway, she sat up, murmuring, "Thanks for driving—I'm really tired."

"I'll get my things and get out of your hair," he said coldly, turning off the ignition and passing her the key.

She walked into the living room ahead of him. His painting, unfinished, was standing on the easel, its luminous hues full of glowing life. Shea gave an exclamation of delight and walked closer, her eyes glued to it.

He was painting Tigger and Minnie in the garden among the poppies and marigolds. The focal point was the dog, his brown eyes leading the viewer's eyes to Minnie and thence to the untidy mass of flowers. Although Simon had only painted Minnie's face and a fraction of the flowers, a soft light suffused the garden, while the close bond between the old woman and the dog was delineated without a trace of sentimentality.

Shea said quietly, "It's magnificent, Simon."

He grunted something in reply, stashing his supplies in a box and putting the panel on the table while he folded up the easel. She said awkwardly, "Where will you paint now?"

"At Jim's apartment in the city." He retrieved the two small oils from the kitchen and put them in the box as well. "Do you mind driving me back to Jim's?"

"Of course not." She bit her lip. "That painting's a huge victory for you."

It was a victory that at the moment tasted like ashes in his mouth. "I had to change from oils to tempera, that was part of the trouble," he said. "Let's go."

"I wish you hadn't fallen in love with me!" she burst out.

"I wish I hadn't, too," he said grimly, picked up the box and headed for the door, kicking it open with one foot.

They drove to Jim's in silence. To Simon's infinite relief he saw that the cabin was deserted; Jim had mentioned that he and Sally might visit some friends in Bridgewater that evening. Shea helped him carry the stuff inside, then said in a strained voice, "Well, good night,

Simon. Thank you again for coming to look for me and for getting me down that tree."

He said flatly, "Goodbye, Shea."

Visibly flinching, she turned and left the cabin. As Simon propped the painting back on the easel, he heard her car back out of the lane. He put the box of gear in his bedroom and went out to sit on the veranda.

He'd gambled and he'd lost.

He'd made the mistake of falling in love with a woman who was afraid of love. Shea had bracketed him in her mind with Tim and Nicholas, two men who had not wanted the real woman but someone who would fit their stereotypes of what a woman should be.

He, Simon, loved her as she was. But Shea was too caught up in the past to know the difference. So she'd turned him down.

And he was damned if he was going to beg her to fall in love with him.

CHAPTER NINE

A WEEK later Simon finished the painting.

He stood back from it, still holding his brush, and without vanity knew it was the best thing he had ever done. The integrity, compassion and sheer life force that he had thought he had lost forever were all there in a rectangular panel two feet by three feet.

He only hoped Minnie would like it. It would be ironic, he thought, if she preferred the two small oils he had done first.

What was even more ironic—and here his mouth tightened—was that in completing a portrait to which he was proud to sign his name he had removed what he had once presumed to be the only barrier between him and Shea.

He had not seen her all week. He had moved into Jim's apartment the day after her rescue, and here he had stayed, driving himself unmercifully to finish the painting. Looking with absentminded satisfaction at the way the sunlight shone through the tissue-paper petals of the poppies, Simon decided that any psychologist worthy of the name would probably call him a better artist for having loved and lost.

He missed Shea continually, sharply, and with an underlying desperation that frightened him. He was not quite sure how he was going to live without her. He had gone as far as to ascertain that there were seats available on the jets flying to London; yet he owed Jim a great deal more than a headlong flight back to England, however much that might seem like the only option in the dark hours of the morning between 2:00 and 4:00 a.m.

He looked at his watch, wondering if he should drive to Somerville now that he was finished. He felt drained and depleted. This was a common enough sensation at the end of any work; but Simon didn't think he had the energy to face the lake and the cabin and the knowledge that the woman he loved was just across that lake. Not tonight.

He spent an hour cleaning his brushes and putting away his supplies, his eyes every now and then straying to the painting. And not even the loss of Shea could entirely quell his inner gratification.

Picking up the phone, he ordered Chinese food to be delivered to the apartment, and had a shower, hoping that the hot water sluicing his body would take away some of his tiredness. Rubbing himself down in the bathroom, he caught sight of the long, jagged scar on his thigh. He would carry it for the rest of his life, he supposed, a constant reminder of Shea.

The buzzer rang. Wrapping a towel around his hips, Simon went to the door, paid for the food and put it on the counter. Then he headed for the bedroom, where he had a clean pair of jeans in his suitcase.

He was halfway there when someone tapped on the door. Perhaps he'd been given the wrong change, he thought, and padded back across the carpet. He swung the door open.

Shea was standing there.

As his heart gave a great leap in his chest, her image burned itself into Simon's brain. She was wearing a slim-fitting jersey dress in moss green with a big gold zip down the front; gold earrings shaped like leaves bumped against her neck, while her hair was loose on her shoulders. But her poise and sophistication were only skin-deep: beneath her makeup she looked like a woman on her way to the scaffold.

Before he could say anything, she stammered his name and walked straight into his arms. The softness of her breasts, the scent of her perfume, the warmth of her cheek against his bare shoulder filled Simon with a shudder of desire. And then she raised her face to be kissed.

He shoved the door shut with his elbow and fastened his mouth on hers with a hunger she more than matched. Her leather bag fell to the floor. Not even stopping to think, he picked her up in his arms and carried her into the bedroom. Throwing her down on the bed, he fell across her, smothering her face, her throat, her hair with kisses. She pulled him closer, so that he was in no doubt that she wanted him as badly as he wanted her, and as she did so the towel loosened about his hips.

He tugged at the gold zip, wanting her to be as exposed to him as he was to her, spreading her dress open and discovering with a shock of delight that she was naked beneath it. As he took the pink tip of her breast in his mouth, she cried out with pleasure; and then with a clumsy haste that inflamed all his senses she tried to haul the dress over her head.

He helped her, tossing the dress to the floor, then sliding his hands along her body, rediscovering the jut of her pelvis and the hollow of her belly, feasting his eyes on the fullness of her ivory breasts. He bent his head for another of those long, drugged kisses, and as he did so her hips began moving under his in a rhythm that made his pulses race. He muttered, "Shea, I've got nothing to protect you."

"I've looked after that," she said. Then with an entrancing mixture of shyness and boldness she ran her hands along the taut arch of his rib cage to his navel, and then lower, watching his face convulse in a pleasure that was like pain. Simon forgot that he had said he wouldn't sleep with her; and ignored the certainty that in taking her he would bind himself yet more strongly to her. He parted her thighs, touching her in that most intimate of places, playing with her until she was panting and writhing on the bed, and only then entering her.

She cried out his name, clasping his hips, and even in the extremity of his own need he could feel an inner throbbing lay claim to her. Fiercely, possessively, he drove into her, knowing he was already on the very brink, and then tumbling over it into that indescribable place which was tinged with death yet was all of life; and which culminated in a peace unlike any he had ever known.

Very gently he lowered his body onto hers, holding her wordlessly, wondering how it could be possible that one man's body could contain so much happiness. Shea looped her arms around his torso, nuzzling his hair-roughened chest with her cheek, and gave a sigh of repletion. She was right not to speak, Simon thought humbly, for there were no words. Only the joy of having the woman he loved in his arms and in his bed.

But eventually he raised his head, leaning his weight on one elbow. "Based on the last ten minutes we'd get a medal for speed if not subtlety," he said.

"I'm not complaining."

The smile left his face. "You came here to seduce me."

Her eyes looked very dark, and full of uncertainty. "Yes," she said.

He remembered the green dress with its convenient zip, and the nakedness of her breasts beneath it. "Did you plan it in cold blood?"

"No! I've had a dreadful week, Simon. I couldn't sleep and I lost my appetite, all I could think about was you." In a low voice she went on, "It was as though I was driven to come here tonight. I couldn't help myself—I had no choice."

He ran his finger along the soft, voluptuous curve of her lip. "You know that I love you."

She nodded. "I know that...but I was so afraid you might go back to England without even telling me."

"I thought of it."

Plucking at the hem of the sheet, she said, "Being here with you—in bed like this—is like flying a helicopter in the dark. All my knowledge is useless to me...I'm relying on intuition."

"Which twice before let you down."

She gave him a small, grateful smile. "Exactly. To continue the metaphor, I crashed."

"I hate that metaphor," Simon said grimly.

"You'd rather I were something safe—a teacher like Sally—wouldn't you?" she flared.

"I didn't say that, Shea," he retorted, the same grimness in his voice. "Flying's part of you, and when I say I love you I mean the whole woman. Your competence and courage—how can I detach those qualities from the rest of you? I can't, and I don't want to. But I'm not going to pretend that I won't worry about you either."

"Oh." For a moment she digested this in silence. Then she raised her head, challenge in her level gaze. "As of midnight I'm on call for forty-eight hours. I might have to leave any time. My beeper's in my handbag."

He ran his finger along the gentle rise of her breast. "Then perhaps we shouldn't waste any time."

Her tiny shiver of pleasure was in no way feigned. But she said, stroking the hard curve of his collarbone, "Actually, I'm very hungry. And I happen to know you ordered Chinese food—that's how I got through the security door downstairs."

"So Chicken Soo Guy takes preference over me?" Simon asked, letting his hand wander lower on her body.

She suddenly grasped his wrist, her face very serious. "Simon, I want you to know that I've never made love like that before...as though I was taken over, overwhelmed, so that I almost didn't know where I ended and you began."

He could lose himself in the cloudy gray of her irises, he thought. "It was the same for me—as though it were the very first time. Are you sure you're not in love with me, Shea?"

She dropped his wrist as if it were a burning ember. "I'm not, I know I'm not," she said incoherently. "Please don't push me, Simon."

What if she never fell in love with him? What then?

With a huge effort of will Simon forced his fears into the background. "We could have Chinese food first and then come back to bed...it's quite a while until midnight."

Her relief was much too evident for his peace of mind. "I like that idea," she said.

He found her one of his shirts and pulled on a pair of shorts, and they went out to the kitchen. But on the way Shea saw the easel standing near the patio doors that led on to Jim's balcony. As though it were a magnet she went over to stand in front of it, her eyes drinking in the finished portrait. For a long time she was silent, long enough for Simon to feel tension gather in his muscles. He had worried that Minnie might not like it. But what if Shea didn't?

She turned to face him, her smile dazzling. "It's wonderful, Simon," she said softly. "I thought it was beautiful before it was finished, but now it's breathtaking. Minnie asked for a painting of Tigger—and you've given her her whole life." Her eyes drawn back to the portrait again, she added, "The way you included those shadows at the back of the garden—that's the death of her husband and Tigger's death too, isn't it? But the flowers, all the joy of life, that's what you see first."

Simon said banally, "I'm glad you like it."

"I'd love to go with you when you give it to her," Shea said wistfully.

He, like Shea, seemed to have no choice. "Of course you can. If it hadn't been for you, I wouldn't have been able to paint it."

She gave him a sudden hard hug. "That painting's really you, I know it is. I'm so happy for you."

To have someone truly rejoice in his accomplishment—particularly a painting that culminated a year of struggle—was a new experience for Simon; one he liked, he thought, hugging Shea back.

They ate on the balcony, which was lit by the gold rays of the setting sun. Then Simon washed some raspberries, opened a package of chocolate cookies and made coffee. Throughout all those prosaic activities he found his gaze returning to Shea over and over again, lingering on the line of her throat, the jut of her breasts under his shirt, the delicate tracery of blue veins at knee and ankle. Despite the painting that was only feet away from him, he knew it was not the artist in him fastening on these details: it was the man.

They moved into the living room with their coffee because the air had cooled as the sun went down. Shea tucked herself into the corner of the sofa, her hands curled around her cup as she made light conversation that belied the growing unease in her eyes. Finishing his coffee, Simon said, "What are you worrying about, Shea? That we've made love so I've got what I wanted, that we've had supper to satisfy the conventions, and that you should probably leave now?"

"You're a mind reader," she said crossly.

"As I keep telling you to the point of boredom, I'm not Tim and I'm not Nicholas." His voice roughened with emotion. "I'm beginning to think it may take a lifetime for me to convince you how much I love you. I'm not going to run away just because you might have to go out flying at some ungodly hour of the morning. Or because sometimes you might be late for dinner."

She blurted, "But you're only here for the summer."

"I'll have to go back to London in a month or so to clean up some business matters. But if Minnie's painting is anything to go by, I can work better here than there." His smile was crooked. "You might be stuck with me."

She said breathlessly, "Let's go back to bed."

She was still running, he thought with a disappointment that was like a stab wound. There was, he supposed, some kind of poetic justice in the fact that he, who had never had to pursue a woman in his life, was now so uncertain of the one woman he had fallen in love with. "Suits me," he said.

This time he made love to her without urgency or haste, savoring each moment, wanting to give to her every gift of his body and soul. And he could see from the wonderment and delight that chased across her features that he was leading her into a place where she had

never been before, a place where her needs were at the
very center of the act. She expanded like a flower to his
touch; and Simon found his reward as she began, shyly
at first, then with increasing confidence, to experiment.
To touch him where she had not touched him before.
To straddle him, riding him as a mermaid rode the wild
sea waves. To show him every nuance of her response,
peeling away the protective covering on her emotions
until they were as naked to him as her pale, graceful
body.

The same fierce storm gathered them in as it had the
first time. But afterward Shea fell asleep in Simon's arms,
her hair falling over his shoulder and her thighs en-
twined with his.

Listening to the soft rise and fall of her breathing, he
reached down to cover her with the sheet. She murmured something under her breath, snuggling closer to
his chest, then growing quiet again. The scent of his skin
had imprinted itself on hers like a primitive seal of
belonging.

Simon was awake for a long time, almost as though
he was afraid that if he fell asleep he would wake to find
her gone from him, a memory elusive as a dream. But
he did sleep—and was woken by a rhythmic, irritating
burr that was like a telephone yet was not one. Beside
him Shea sat bolt upright. "The beeper," she gasped.
"Where did I leave my purse?"

Not waiting for an answer, she scrambled out of bed
and ran from the bedroom. Simon rubbed at the stubble
on his chin, noticing that the first pale light of dawn
was just creeping in behind the curtains. He heard the
mechanical rasp of the message, then a moment or two
later Shea was speaking on the kitchen telephone.
"Yes...sure...I'll be there by six-thirty." Then she

hurried back into the bedroom. "Simon, while I get in the shower, please could you throw on some clothes and get my bag out of my car? It's parked on the street just outside the main door."

He said calmly, "Yes—if you give me a kiss first."

She was stooping to pick up her clothes. "I haven't got long. There's a big fire broken out about forty miles from Somerville, the woods are tinder-dry and the weather bureau isn't even bothering to forecast rain any more."

"Shea," Simon said cogently, "the forest will not burn down in the time it'll take you to give me a kiss."

"I need my bag," she repeated impatiently. "My flying suit's in it."

He got out of bed in one swift movement, his nude body looming over hers in the dimly lit room. "Maybe the reason Tim and Nicholas had trouble with your job is because you turned them off like a light switch the minute someone phoned you from the depot. I'll have trouble with——"

"Simon," Shea said tightly, "I don't have the time to argue right now. If you won't get my bag, then I will."

She was wrestling with the green dress, which was inside out. "You're not listening to me," Simon said with dangerous precision. "I'm perfectly happy to get your bag and I understand that you have to leave. What I don't like is being treated like a piece of furniture only hours after we made love!"

"You don't have to shout," she said coldly, pulling on her brief lacy underwear, the sinuous movements of her body igniting a desire for her so imperative that Simon might never have made love to her. Then she reached for the dress.

He took her by the shoulders, the silken feel of her skin infuriating him. "Go have your shower," he ordered. "I'll get your bag. But we're not finished with this."

She glared at him and marched out of the room. "The keys are in my purse," she snapped, and pulled the bathroom door shut behind her.

Simon put on shorts and the shirt Shea had been wearing, his senses further excoriated by the faint fragrance of her perfume that clung to the fabric. He then went downstairs and got her overnight bag. When he arrived back in the apartment, she was still in the bathroom. He said shortly, "Your bag's outside the door," and went into the kitchen to brew some coffee.

A few minutes later she joined him there, looking very trim in her flying suit, her hair in a single braid. "I won't have time for coffee," she said with an obvious effort to sound pleasant. "I'll get some at the depot before I take off." Dutifully she raised her face for a kiss. "Bye, Simon."

He stood still, making no attempt to kiss her. "We made love last night, Shea. For the first time. I won't be fobbed off as if I'm a casual acquaintance you only just met."

Her breath hissed between her teeth. "I can't mix my job with all this emotion," she cried. "I have to keep them separate, don't you understand that?"

"I understand that the worst thing we could be doing is quarreling before you have to fly. And I do see that you can't be daydreaming about me when you're at the controls of a helicopter, especially if a forest fire is burning underneath you. But I'm goddamned if keeping your job and your emotions separate means treating me as if I don't exist. Don't *you* understand *that*?"

He seemed to have run out of words. "I don't know what I understand any more," Shea said desperately. "I don't even understand myself! I've got to go, I'm going to be late."

She fled from the kitchen. Simon took one step after her, watching her pick up her bag and cross the living room. At the door to the apartment she hesitated briefly. Then she tossed her head and went out into the hall. The door clicked shut behind her.

He could have stopped her. He could have pulled her into his arms and kissed her until she couldn't breathe. But what was the use?

She hadn't heard a word he'd said.

The next afternoon Sally called Simon up from the wharf where he was lying in the sun after a long swim. "Someone at the helicopter depot wants to speak to you," she said as he climbed up the path.

His steps missed a beat. Wondering if he would ever get over an initial pang of fear from such phone calls, hoping it hadn't shown in his face, he went inside, picked up the phone and said hello.

"Bill Dugan here, Simon. Just a minute, Shea's coming on the line."

Then Simon heard Shea's voice, sounding artificial and very far away. "Simon? I have to go to Halifax to take a little boy to the children's hospital. I could meet you for a quick supper if you were interested. I don't imagine I'll be back at the cabin for several days."

Simon knew very well that this was a peace offering. "Where and when?" he said crisply.

She named a restaurant near the hospital. "At five? I'll have to get back to the fire site by dark."

Simon and Jim had already decided to join the ground crew the next day; but for some reason he didn't want to tell Shea that. "I'll be there," he said. "Safe journey, Shea."

"Thanks. See you."

He hung up and told Sally his plans. Sally was obviously pleased; Sally wanted everyone to be as happy as she was. "You'll have to take the car, because Jim's got the truck," she said, her brow furrowing. "There was something needed checking on it, but I'm darned if I can remember what."

"I'm sure it'll be okay," Simon said. Although mechanical things weren't his brother's speciality, the car, despite various squeals and rattles, always seemed to get Jim where he wanted to go.

He dressed in record time. The car started at the first touch of the ignition and charged out of the driveway, the choke flooding the engine as it nearly always did. But on the highway it settled down. Simon soon decided it was the muffler that needed checking; hoping it wouldn't fall off before he reached Halifax, he drove steadily toward the city, his hands taut on the wheel.

He had underestimated the depth of Shea's conflict between her job and her private life. But he was not prepared to retract one single statement that he had made that morning. He'd gladly give her time to learn to trust him; what he wouldn't do was act as though he were a nonentity the minute the telephone rang.

Another battle of wills, he thought, and wondered how long it would take Shea to put her trust in him.

He was twenty minutes outside the city when the car started pulling persistently to one side. He wrestled with the wheel for a minute or two, then eased over onto the hard shoulder, stopped and got out. A flat tire on the passenger side.

Cursing under his breath, he unearthed the jack and the spare tire in the trunk. He'd learned to call it the trunk and not the boot, he thought, looking down at his pristine white pants before kneeling on the ground. Oh, well, Shea would probably be in her flying suit; perhaps it wasn't too high-class a restaurant.

When he had the front jacked up, he heaved the spare out onto the ground; then, his jaw set, his feelings less than friendly toward his brother, he saw that the spare, too, was flat. It took him ten minutes to flag down a car, another ten to drive to the nearest service station, and a further twenty to wait for the proprietor, an old man called Jethro who was as cheerful as he was dirty, to get around to fixing the tire. To Simon's inquiry about a telephone the old man cackled that it was out of order. "Waitin' for me to pay my bill, they are," he said, spitting with careless accuracy into the pit. "I'm not so hot on the paperwork, but do those danged office workers understand that? No sirree. They just want their money. Trouble with this country is that the ones runnin' it ain't got no sense of humour."

Wishing he could have phoned the restaurant, Simon waited as patiently as he could. Fortunately the old man was better at fixing tires than at paying his bills; they were soon on their way back to Jim's car in a tow truck whose motor purred like a charm and whose interior was so filthy that Simon was perversely fascinated. The tire was replaced in record time, money changed hands, and with an amiable grin Jethro drove away.

Simon, by now over an hour late, drove to the city as fast as he dared. The traffic was heavy and he had trouble finding a parking lot. The restaurant, which was charmingly decorated like a French café, was nearly full. He searched among the tables for a woman with tawny hair and gray eyes, and although he attracted several interested glances none of them belonged to Shea.

The hostess, in an abbreviated black dress, said politely, "Are you looking for someone, sir?"

"Yes. A woman in a beige flying suit, blonde hair, she should have arrived here over an hour ago." He added the obvious. "I'm late."

"I remember her. But she didn't arrive until about twenty minutes ago. When she saw you weren't here, she left."

So Shea had been late herself. With lightning speed Simon guessed what had happened. Shea had been delayed. When she had finally arrived at the restaurant she had jumped to the conclusion that he, Simon, had not bothered waiting for her. So the flat tire had inadvertently played into the worst of her fears.

"Thanks," he said briefly, left the restaurant, and ran across the street. The hospital was only a few blocks away; with any luck Shea might have stopped there for something to eat. All hospitals had cafeterias, didn't they?

The cafeteria was crowded, but empty of the one woman he wanted; and the commissionaire at the front desk told him the helicopter had left a quarter of an hour ago.

While Simon was furious with the series of mishaps that had made him so late, he was equally furious with Shea for not waiting. For the second time in less than forty-eight hours she'd allowed her job to come between them. She hadn't trusted him, that was the crux of the matter. Instead she had instantly assumed he was a carbon copy of all the other men she'd known.

They were headed for a showdown, he thought, his mouth a thin line. Because he wasn't going to spend the rest of his life chasing after her in restaurants. He strode out of the hospital, found a pavement café where with minimal appetite he ate very good seafood chowder and spinach salad, and went back to Jim's car. Which, of course, behaved perfectly all the way home.

CHAPTER TEN

THE next morning Simon and Jim drove the truck to the fire site. The base camp was in a community hall that was equipped with a kitchen. The fire boss, whose name was Chester, had taken over the stage, while the big main room was split between dining room and dormitory. Wondering where Shea slept, Simon dumped his gear and discovered that he and Jim were both assigned to building a firebreak.

He never forgot that day. If he had found his first fire awe-inspiring, this one was frankly terrifying. A hot, dry wind fanned the flames so that they leaped into the roiling clouds of smoke with deadly grace, springing from tree to tree with every wayward gust. The heat was intense, the noise deafening, the acrid smoke overpowering.

Simon used a chain saw the entire day, backing up the bulldozers that were shoving the undergrowth and boulders into a makeshift fire road. The first ten minutes he had to battle with the unpleasant memories of the last time he had used a chain saw; after that, the sheer physical demands and the proximity of the fire drove lesser concerns from his mind.

By the time he and Jim stopped for lunch, Simon was soaked with sweat, every muscle in his body screaming a protest. A week of portrait painting was not the way to limber up for fire fighting, he thought ruefully, putting his hard hat on the bank and wiping his forehead. However, as the other men arrived to eat, Steve and Joe greeted him with genuine pleasure; and the meal was punctuated by the regular overhead passes of two helicopters, the Bell and Shea's blue one.

After he had eaten, he lay back in the sweet-scented ferns for a fifteen-minute nap that gave him a second wind. They took a coffee break about five, then worked until dusk, joined by a local band of firemen whose long hoses soaked the woods on the far side of the firebreak. Through the billowing smoke the setting sun was as red as blood. As the wind gradually quietened the flames sank lower, the fire falling asleep like a great animal that at any moment could be roused to life: dangerous, unpredictable, full of ire.

When they got back to the base camp the crew were told that showers were available in the local schoolhouse just up the road, a bonus at the end of a day that Simon, at least, had found exhausting. He shucked off his boots and hung his orange suit and hard hat on the hooks in the vestibule, catching sight of his dirt-encrusted face in the mirror. His T-shirt was clinging to his chest and he would not want to be downwind of his socks.

He had to pass through the dining room to get clean clothes from his duffle bag. He saw Shea immediately, chatting to Michael partway across the room. Michael waved at him. Shea looked up, still smiling at something the other pilot had said. As if she were an actress in a silent film, the smile was wiped from her face. Her fork clattered onto her plate.

Simon didn't want to talk to her now, when he was dirty and hungry and tired. What he had to say would keep.

He edged past the curtain into the dormitory, found his clean clothes, and went for a shower. Washing the grime from his body seemed like utter luxury; never again would he take such simple things as soap and water for granted, he decided, rinsing the shampoo from his hair.

He had dinner with Steve, Joe, Charlie and Jim. Shea was now involved in an animated game of cards with two other crews. Presumably she thought that surrounding herself with men would keep him at a distance, he thought, eating his roast turkey. He took his time over the meal, enjoying the lemon meringue pie and coffee that followed the turkey. Then he got up and sauntered over to the card game.

He watched for several minutes until he was sure he had the rules down pat. Then he squeezed his chair in directly across from Shea. She gave him a cool nod and proceeded to ignore him. All right, thought Simon, accepting cards from the dealer, if that's the way you want to play it, I'll see what I can do to make you notice me.

His natural flair for cards had been honed first by his mother and then by the gang with whom he had traveled when he was ten. Very deliberately he set out to defeat Shea as often as he could, nor did he bother to be subtle about his tactics. She caught on very fast; her cheeks grew pinker, her eyes stormier as he trumped her aces and took trick after trick. Although she was too good a player to go down without a fight, Simon's play was inspired, and, as could happen, he was dealt a run of extremely good cards.

In the final hand he wiped her out with a wild card. There was an indrawn hiss of breath from the watching crew, who could not fail to have been aware of what was going on. Into the silence Simon said, "I'd like a word with Shea—in private." He ran his eyes around the group of men. "If you wouldn't mind."

With one accord the men got to their feet and melted into the background, leaving Shea and Simon isolated in a sea of chairs. Shea said in a choked whisper, "How dare you humiliate me like that? I have to work with these men."

"So do I." He gave her a lazy grin, leaning back in his chair and hooking his thumbs in his belt like the cowboy heroes he had admired when he was a boy. "You're not a bad card player."

Her knuckles tightened on the edge of the table. "I don't have to stay here and listen to this."

Like a whiplash his voice cut the air between them. "Stay put, Shea. There's something I have to say to you."

She sank back in her chair, her cheeks now white with fury. "What is this, macho stuff? I'll-show-you-who's-the-boss? I thought you were a cut above that, Simon."

"Apparently not. You walked out on me the other morning, now it's my turn to set the rules."

"There's no game," she spat, "so there aren't any rules. You *are* like Tim and Nicholas—you didn't wait for me yesterday at the restaurant. I was forty-five minutes late because the 'copter——"

"Shea," he interrupted, dropping the front legs of his chair on the floor and leaning across the table, "I had a flat tire. I was over an hour late myself."

As her eyes widened, he could almost see the calculations flitting through her brain. Before she could speak, he pushed on, "Jim's spare was flat as well and I was five miles from a garage. A very entertaining old gent by the name of Jethro fixed the tire, in the meantime telling me how the country should be run. I got to the restaurant twenty minutes after you'd left, and when I went straight to the hospital you'd already gone."

She said faintly, "It never occurred to me that you might have been late."

"That's obvious." Remorselessly Simon moved to the attack. "You didn't trust me, did you? As soon as you saw I wasn't there, you jumped to the conclusion that I couldn't handle the demands of your job and you flew back to the base. Did you even ask the hostess if I'd been there?"

She shook her head. "I didn't think there was any point."

Ruthlessly he pressed his advantage. "This is about trust, Shea. Heaven knows a relationship between you and me isn't going to be easy, we're both too strong-willed for that . . . but if we don't trust each other we're defeated before we start."

"Who says we've started?" she demanded.

"You came to Jim's apartment the other night."

Her eyes fell. "Yes, I did, didn't I? My father always told me to think before I act."

Her words sliced through his composure. "Are you saying you're sorry you went to the apartment? Sorry we made love?"

"No, I'm not saying that!" She rested her hand on his arm in unconscious pleading, her words tumbling over one another. "But I didn't anticipate where it would lead me, I didn't think ahead to how it would put you and my job on a collision course—I didn't think at all!"

"They don't have to collide—they can coexist," he said with all the force of his willpower.

"I wish I could believe that," she whispered.

"You've got to trust me, Shea—you can't run away every time you think I've let you down." Hurt raw in his voice, he added, "And you can't treat me like some chance-met stranger the minute the depot phones."

"I know I behaved badly the morning I was on call. I didn't know how else to handle it."

"One kiss—even a fairly leisurely one—would not have altered the course of this fire one iota. And it would have made me feel a hell of a lot better."

"Me too," she said in a small voice. "I felt awful the rest of the day. That's why I phoned you yesterday."

Her honesty, combined with the vulnerable droop of her mouth, touched him to the core; the last of his anger fell away. "I think I'll kiss you right now," he said. "Just to make up for lost time."

She gave her surroundings a quick survey; as she did so, heads snapped around and the buzz of conversation picked up appreciably. "You've done enough damage," she said forbiddingly. "They've probably been listening to every word."

He stood up and walked around the table. "I want them all to know that you belong to me," he said.

Swiftly she got to her feet, her eyes wary. "You're like a bulldozer, Simon," she said, "flattening everything in your path."

"Let's start a backfire, then," he said, cupping her face in his hands and smiling down at her.

"Your eyes are so blue," she said crossly, "they're absolutely gorgeous, and you'd better darn well be prepared for the consequences if you kiss me."

He was openly laughing. "Are you daring me again? That's not very clever of you."

"Backfires sometimes start a forest fire of their own. Didn't they teach you that on your course?"

"Some kinds of conflagration they didn't cover," he murmured, and bent his head to kiss her.

It was neither a brief nor a particularly chaste kiss; when Simon eventually released Shea there was a moment of appreciative silence then a chorus of wolf whistles and clapping. Shea dropped a mock curtsy in her soot-stained flying suit and sat down again. Her cheeks were very pink. Riffling the pack of cards between her fingers, she said, "What do we do for an encore?"

"We can't. Not here."

"Too bad."

"We'd both better pray for rain," he said tersely, sitting down and taking the cards from her. "In the meantime I'll teach you some of my mother's card tricks."

The other men gradually drifted back to watch, and it was after midnight before the dormitory settled down. Shea was sleeping in a spartan little dressing room off the stage; Simon's good-night kiss was reasonably restrained. He murmured, for her ears alone, "Repeat ten times before you go to sleep—Simon is not Tim or Nicholas. Got that?"

"If you hadn't been late yesterday, you would have waited for me..."

"Yes."

She sighed. "Trust is a big word."

"Trust and love," he said, "two of the biggest there are."

He took the memory of her perplexed face to his narrow little cot. He woke before dawn, and was instantly wide awake in a way that made it useless to stay in bed. He crept out of the dormitory and went outside.

The fire was five miles down the road; through the trees Simon could smell the pall of smoke. He was suddenly struck with how far he had traveled in the last couple of months, from his London studio and his comfortable Sussex cottage to a threatened wilderness and a woman who was afraid to trust him, let alone love him. He sat down on the stone step, glad to have a few minutes to himself.

He might have been there for quarter of an hour when he heard someone running across the grass toward the building. As he got up and looked around the corner, Shea stopped in her tracks only a few feet away from him. "What are you doing up?" she said.

She was wearing faded jeans and a pink T-shirt, her hair hanging in damp ringlets, and she was breathing hard, as though she had run all the way from the showers. His eyes narrowed. "What's wrong, Shea?" he asked, and stepped closer.

Looking flustered, she said, "Oh, nothing. I——"

There was a circle of red marks on her upper arm, as though she had been held too tightly. "Who's been bothering you?" he rapped.

Scowling, she said reluctantly, "It was Everett. He——"

"*Everett's* here?"

She nodded. "He's not staying in the dorm because he's got relatives in the village. He was hanging around the showers when I got out... Simon, murder's against the law, and I got rid of him on my own."

Trying to quell a rage that indeed felt murderous, Simon said, "Where is he now?"

"I have no idea and I wouldn't tell you if I had. I told him if he ever came around me again I'd set the police on him for throwing that boulder down the hill. It scared him enough that he backed off."

"The next time I see him I'll give him the same message," Simon said with deadly calm, "but he'll be flat on his back. Did he hurt you?"

"He scared me, that's all. Simon, why are we talking about Everett when by some miracle we might have five minutes alone together?"

He pushed Everett to the back of his mind. "Trying to seduce me again?" he asked.

"Five minutes isn't long enough for that."

"We could make a start." He drew her into his arms, gently tracing the red marks with his finger then bending his head and kissing the bruised skin with all the tenderness that she evoked in him. She rested one hand on his thick dark hair and said shakily, "I never know what you're going to do next."

When he looked up there were tears in her eyes. "I love you, Shea," he said, and wondered if he was tempting the gods to love one woman as much as he loved this one.

As though she had read his mind she said with sudden urgency, "You be careful today, won't you? I don't like this fire. It has a bad feel to it."

The pungent smell of smoke was surrounding them both. He gave her a quick kiss. "Let's go in and get a coffee," he suggested, knowing he craved people and noise and confusion rather than the preternatural dawn silence. Not even the birds were singing, he thought with a superstitious *frisson* along his spine.

After breakfast Shea went outside to supervise refueling and Simon's crew was given new instructions by the fire boss. "I'm shifting all you guys to the other flank along with another crew—there's a big hunting lodge there we want to save." He showed them the layout of the land on the aerial map. "The fire road's through here—you'll work this side, and the helicopters will water-bomb as close as they can get. Keep in touch with your crew boss all the time, got that?" He folded the map. "Good luck."

The other crew was at the site ahead of them; one of its members was Everett. The look of dismay on his face when he saw Simon might have been funny in other circumstances. Simon could feel his fists bunch at his sides, and he had to make a conscious effort to listen to Steve's instructions. Everett would be around all day; there was no hurry.

What had looked relatively straightforward on the fire boss's map was by no means so simple on the ground, which was littered with granite boulders and traversed by gullies thigh-deep with ferns. The men worked at widening the fire road and keeping the woods surrounding the lodge and its storage sheds as wet as they could; the fire had veered in the other direction because of a change in the wind, so the work seemed easy to Simon in comparison with the day before. They ate lunch beside a lake whose far shore was charred from the fire, Everett sitting as far from Simon as he could.

Simon had just tossed his apple core into the trees when the surface of the lake broke into riffles and his T-shirt was suddenly flattened to his back. Steve said apprehensively, "The wind's changed direction. We'd better soak her down some more, fellas. Let's go."

The lodge was in sight of the lake, the fire road a few hundred feet on the other side of it. The owner of the lodge had cut down some of the trees, so that the remaining clumps of fir and spruce were tall and well-shaped, very green in the dull, eerie light that penetrated the smoke. The sun had a halo around it; the air was so hot and dry that Simon's skin felt tight across his cheekbones.

As he tramped over the rough terrain with a loaded water pump strapped to his back, bracken and brittle dead branches crunched underfoot. Ready-made kindling, he thought edgily, wondering if it was his imagination that the flames were already closer. The wind was

'anning his cheeks—a wind that should have been cooling
ind was not.

The blue helicopter flew overhead, the rhythmic beat
of its rotors as familiar to him as breathing. It dumped
ts bucket of water along the fire road north of the lodge,
hen circled back through the smoke to reload in the
ake. Obscurely comforted to know Shea was so close,
Simon scrambled down the gully between the lake and
he buildings. The lichen on the rocks crackled like paper.
The sharp tang of smoke was stronger now, carried on
he breeze; he was sure it must have penetrated his very
pores.

He was following a long hose from the lake as it snaked
over the ground. When he reached the farthermost shed,
ie and Jim angled the jet of water on the strip of land
between it and the road. Over the loud hiss of the hose
im yelled, "Steve wanted more of those trees cut
lown—you be okay here?"

Everett was already felling the spruce between the
econd shed and the lodge. Everett, give him his due,
vas a steady worker, Simon thought dryly. Too bad the
est of his behavior was so obnoxious.

The hose was awkward and very heavy; Simon's
houlders were soon aching from the strain as he swished
he water back and forth over the undergrowth, and then
over the buildings themselves. A new sound was as-
erting itself over the snarl of the saws and the jet of
vater: the dull roar of flames, the very voice of the fire.
His mouth dry, Simon watched the curtain of brilliant
olor that was approaching the far side of the road,
lancing and leaping through the treetops, the smoke
hurning skyward with a life of its own.

No road ever built could stop that, he thought.

Its blades juddering, the blue helicopter made its drop so close to him that a few moments later a cool sprinkle of water landed on his face. He thought of Shea and in sudden excitement knew that his next portrait would be of her. But not the woman of the lake, naked among the lilies. Rather the Shea of the forest fires, her gray eyes like smoke, her passion the orange leap of flames, her hair blown in the wind...

He gazed at the scene in front of him, abstracted from its danger to see only its wild and terrible beauty, his eyes noting detail after detail. Flame writhing around a tree, gathering it into a lethal embrace. The incredible range of hues in the roiling smoke: yellow, orange, blue, black, gray. Everything in motion, nothing still.

Absently he braced himself and directed the hose to the roof of the next shed, wishing he had his hands free to sketch some of the impressions so vivid in his mind. Then he was brought back to reality as Jim came running up to him, brushing sweat from his face. "Steve wants us to pull back at the first sign that the fire's crossing the road," he shouted. "They'll be turning the pump off at the lake, and two of us'll haul the hose back to the truck. If there's time, cut down the trees nearest the lodge." His brown eyes very serious, he added, "Don't fool with this one, Simon—you looked as if you were a hundred miles away."

Simon's grin split his dirty face. "Just worked out my next painting. But I hear you—I'll keep my mind on the job from now on."

"You do that. This isn't a tidy little bonfire on Guy Fawkes Day—this is for real."

Jim hurried off to warn Everett, and Simon concentrated on his task. While he had been daydreaming the fire had marched closer, a mighty, unstoppable army destroying everything in its path. A fierce gust of wind pushed against his chest, ashes peppering his overalls and the smoke making his eyes water. The flames, bright-fingered and greedy, were already clutching at the trees on the far side of the road, transforming all their verdant fullness into stark, blackened skeletons.

For a moment Simon was gripped by sheer terror. He was like a field mouse trying to halt a herd of buffalo, he thought, his nerves as taut as overstressed wire. The fire, maddened by its own energy, cared nothing for him. He was no more to it than a tree or a rock.

Then, to his right, he saw that the fire was at the very edge of the bulldozed road, a wall of sinuous flame thwarted because it found nothing new to devour. For a minute or two it looked as though the barrier would hold. With a wild lift of his spirits Simon thought that the men had won and the fire was defeated.

But the wind, itself created by the searing heat, was driving the orange plumes high into the air in a frenzied, demonic dance. In an elegant pirouette a tongue of fire touched the very tip of a tree on Simon's side of the road. The treetop exploded into flame, then the next tree caught and the next.

Simultaneously the water pressure in the hose lessened. When he looked back over his shoulder, Jim was waving at him. Simon hauled the nozzle from between the two sheds, freeing it up to be reeled in, and went to get his chain saw. Then everything happened very fast.

A great blast of wind and a surge of smoke flung themselves between him and the rest of the crew, so that Jim vanished as if he had never been. The same wind carried flames light as feathers to land in the trees Everett had not yet felled, and sparks that sizzled and spat on the wet roof. From behind him he heard a fierce

crackling. He whirled, seeing to his horror that the far
shed had already been engulfed by the blaze. Dimly he
heard someone shout a warning and turned back. The
roof of the nearer shed had caught, he saw with an almost
detached sense of fatality; Everett was running toward
him, jumping from rock to rock with an agility he had
to admire.

"We gotta get outa here!" Everett yelled, his grammar
deteriorating under stress. "This ain't no time to stand
around admirin' the view."

Simon scarcely had time to realize that Everett could
well have left him to his fate when a new sound cut
through the cacophony of the fire. A sound like fire-
works exploding, a sharp staccato volley. Then something whizzed past his cheek, so close that he felt the
wind of its passing. Everett shrieked with pain and
crumpled to the ground in an untidy heap.

Simon flung himself down. Bullets, he thought,
crawling as fast as he could through the tangled underbrush toward the fallen man, adrenaline pumping
through his veins. This is a hunting lodge. Someone's
left ammunition in the shed and it's exploding in the
heat.

He was already fumbling for the first-aid kit that he
now carried in his waist pack; that it was there was entirely due to the accident with the chain saw, an irony
he fervently hoped Everett was still alive to appreciate.
The shots had ceased. He turned Everett over. A pulse
was fluttering at the base of his throat; Everett was unconscious, not dead, Simon realized with deep relief, his
mouth twisting wryly as he recalled his murderous rage
earlier that morning.

There was a spreading stain like a red blossom on the
shoulder of Everett's overalls. Simon hurriedly pushed

a pad on the wound and bound it into place, aware of heat scorching the back of his neck, and praying that there was no ammunition in the shed that was starting to burn only feet away from him. Then he looked up.

All the landmarks he had subconsciously grown used to in the last few hours were gone, wreathed in smoke and flame. Right in front of him an alder bush was burning, each branch a limb of fire upheld in graceful abandon. The blast of heat from the flames pulsing through the windows of the shed hit him like a blow. He had to get out of here, he thought frantically, striving for a sense of direction in a landscape altered beyond belief.

He heaved Everett's body across his shoulder and pushed himself upright, staggering from the man's weight. His boots skidding among the rocks, he lurched into the open space behind the sheds. With a grunt of dismay he saw that the trees that fringed the lake were wrapped in flame, a sheet of fire that cut off any possibility of him reaching the safety of the water.

The gully. He'd have to cross the gully into the next clearing. Almost running across the grounds of the lodge, terrified that he might sprain an ankle, Simon felt the fumes sear his throat. Panting for breath, he wondered numbly if he was going to die here, burned alive trying to save a man he would have said he hated. For it was quite clear to Simon that he could run three times as fast without his burden; and equally clear that he could never live with himself afterward were he to abandon Everett.

A swirl of smoke surrounded him in choking gray folds and a red-hot ember struck his cheekbone. With an inchoate cry of pain he brushed it away. Hunched low, he ploughed on, holding a picture of the topography in his mind and battling down a mindless panic that would destroy him if he gave it free rein. He couldn't succumb to panic. If he did, Everett would die, too.

Then, from nowhere, Shea's name suddenly dropped into his mind, and an image filled his vision of her sleek, wet body playing in the cool waters of the lake. Holding her name like a talisman against panic and death, he thought, I can't die. Not yet. Because I've got to convince Shea that she wants to spend the rest of her life with me.

Shea, who holds the very essence of my life in her hands. Shea, whom I love.

CHAPTER ELEVEN

WITH unpredictable and uncaring ease the wind blew the smoke away. The gully was right in front of Simon. Its far rim was ablaze, the shrubs burning like torches against the horizon. He scrambled down the ravine with a speed that would have been out of the question in cold blood, and for a blessed moment or two inhaled cool air at its base. Then, taking a deep breath, he forged up the slope, grasping for handholds, pulling himself up by brute force, sure that his heart was going to burst out of his chest.

Flames licked at the legs of his overalls. He beat at them with his sleeve, almost dropping Everett in the process. Wrestling with the man's inert weight, knowing that he was nearing the end of his strength, Simon saw with blank horror that he was encircled by fire. The trees along the shore, the spruce groves to his right, the shrubs on the distant side of the clearing were all ignited. It would take only a gust of wind to bring the flames inward through the grass and underbrush. He gripped Everett tighter, the roar of the blaze beating against his eardrums. His only chance was to head for the lake and hope that he could burst through the barrier of fire into the water.

If not, he and Everett were dead men.

And then he heard another sound, a sound that snapped his head up. Through the tumultuous clouds of smoke the blue helicopter appeared, a miraculous fragment of reality in a world gone mad. Simon staggered farther into the clearing, wondering if his orange suit was even visible, and saw the machine dip toward him. Shea was seated at the controls. As she made a slow pass overhead she released the water from the bucket, drenching the clearing, soaking Simon's suit and plastering his hair to his face. At the end of her run the bucket fell free of the belly of the helicopter, landing with a dull thump on the ground fifty feet from Simon. Then the helicopter made a tight turn and he could see Shea searching for a level place to land.

It had been one thing to think that he and Everett might die; quite another to fear for Shea's life. His chest tight in an agony of suspense, he watched as she lowered the machine into the center of the clearing. The downdraught thrust against his body; fighting it, he hitched Everett's body higher on his shoulder and ran for the helicopter. The doors were all off, he noticed, his brain working very clearly, knowing that such a small detail could mean the difference between life and death for all three of them.

The draught was fanning the circle of flames to greater fury. Crouching low under the rotor blades, Simon shoved Everett onto the floor behind the front seats and clambered in after him. "Okay," he yelled, falling on top of the other man and grabbing for the metal legs of the seats to anchor himself. With a velocity like a high-speed lift Shea lifted off. As his stomach swooped, Simon caught a glimpse, frighteningly close, of the thwarted flames; then he closed his eyes, holding on with all his remaining strength.

He could hear Shea shouting something. She was flying dead level; he reached with one hand for the nearest headset and hitched it over his ears. "Thanks," he said hoarsely. "That's as close as I ever want to get."

"What's wrong with Everett?"

"Bullet wound in the shoulder. Ammunition exploded in one of the sheds."

"I'll radio ahead for an ambulance. Jim and the others got out by truck." She called the fire boss. Her voice was as calm as if she were ordering Chinese food, Simon thought dazedly. He hadn't spared a thought for his brother since the blaze had leaped the firebreak. Jim must be out of his mind with worry.

A few minutes later Shea started her descent. "Hold on," she said over the intercom. "I'll be as careful as I can."

Simon wanted to tell her that he had absolute trust in her; but somehow he couldn't get the words out. Forcing himself to concentrate, he hunched his weight over Everett to hold him down and clutched the metal bars.

He didn't even feel the landing. The first he knew that he was on the ground was Shea's voice saying, "You can let go now, Simon—we're back at the base."

Simon looked up. A police officer was standing only a foot away from him, his lips moving without any sound. Clumsily Simon took off the headset. "There's an ambulance on its way," the policeman bellowed. "Can you get out?"

Simon got to his knees, his limbs as weak as a newborn infant's. When he backed out of the helicopter, hands gripped him from behind and thrust him down on the grass. He hung his head low, wondering if he was going to faint. Pretty silly thing to do now that it was all over...

Someone pressed a wet cloth to his forehead, and the policeman held out a bottle of water. Simon tipped his head back and took a long drink. The helicopter blades slowed over his head, then Shea jumped down to the ground. She knelt beside him. "Simon, are you hurt?" she said urgently.

He shook his head. Although she was pale, she looked very composed. He wanted to take her in his arms, but his body was trembling with reaction and he was breathing in short, shallow gasps that sent sharp pains through his chest. Fleetingly she clasped his shoulder with a strength he would not have thought she possessed. Then, just as quickly, she released him and said crisply, "I have to file my report—I'll be back in a minute."

Its siren wailing, the ambulance arrived, and Everett was loaded onto a stretcher. With a screech of brakes a truck pulled up behind the ambulance. The first one out of the truck was Jim. His eyes glued to the recumbent, orange-clad form on the stretcher, he ran toward it. And finally Simon found his voice. "Jim," he croaked, "I'm over here."

Jim's head swung around. He looked ghastly, his eyes like pits in a face drained of color. Stumbling over the grass, he ducked under the blades and fell on his knees by his brother. "I thought you were dead," he gabbled. "They wouldn't let me go back for you when we realized you and Everett were missing... I nearly went crazy; it took three of them to hold me down. We didn't know you were alive until Shea got on the radio."

If ever Simon had needed proof that his brother loved him, he had it. He put an arm around Jim's shoulders. "She saved my life," he muttered.

"I had a gut feeling this fire was bad news right from the start. Maybe you should go in the ambulance and get checked over, Simon—you don't look so good."

"I'm all right," Simon said. "I've got to talk to Shea."

The ambulance drove off and Jim got Simon to his feet. They walked around for a few minutes while

Simon's legs gradually returned to normal. His eyes were smarting and his throat hurt; the burn on his cheek throbbed as though someone were holding a hot iron to it. He was, he knew, incredibly lucky.

He had been looking around for Shea, expecting to see her emerge from the building at any minute. Finally he said, "I need to find Shea, Jim...I haven't really thanked her yet."

Jim said rapidly, "I'd never have forgiven myself if you'd died in that fire, Simon. It was because of me that you were there in the first place. Because of me that you're even in the country."

Simon straightened, feeling every muscle in his back and shoulders protest. "Jim," he said in a cracked voice, "I came of my own choice. You and Shea have been the saving of me." He wanted to say more, to tell his brother that he, Simon, had become an automaton in England, out of touch with his feelings, painting beautiful portraits which had no soul. To say that he didn't know what was going to happen in the next few weeks, but that he was a better man for loving his brother and loving the woman who less than an hour ago had saved his life.

But perhaps something in his face had said it for him; he watched Jim swallow, and as his brother's arm went around him he felt salt tears sting his own eyes. "You don't need to go back at the end of the summer," Jim said. "Stay all winter if you want. Stay the rest of your life."

"If Shea will marry me, I might just do that."

"I figured that's the way the wind was blowing—you'd better go find her." Jim clapped him on the back, his teeth very white in his soot-black face. "Good luck."

Simon went inside the building, heading for the fire boss. Shea was nowhere to be seen. The door of her little room was ajar and the room empty. Chester was talking to a crew on the radio; sure that he could hear the roar of flames through the voices, Simon waited until Chester was finished then said abruptly, "Where's Shea?"

"You okay, Simon? Hear you had a close call—you did real well to get Everett out."

"I'm all right," Simon said again. "Where did Shea go?"

The radio crackled and a voice said, "Patrol four calling fire boss. Over."

Chester reached for the microphone. "She went out the back door," he said. "You get that burn on your face looked at."

There was a door leading outside from the back of the stage. Simon stumbled down the steps and walked out into the sunshine. The helicopter was still parked on the grass, so Shea couldn't have gone far. Standing in the shade, he watched the breeze stir the tops of the slender birch trees which grew behind the building.

He hoped to God she wasn't avoiding him.

His steps almost soundless in the grass, he walked along the line of trees until a dip in the land hid the helicopter and the trucks from view. The men's voices faded into the background to be replaced by the fluting call of a thrush somewhere in the forest. He walked a little farther, all his senses alert. Maybe she wasn't this way at all. Maybe she'd headed for the showers.

Then a new sound reached his ears. He stood still, listening intently, and saw with a quiver of excitement that there was a narrow path edged with ferns leading into the woods. He started down it, trying to be quiet, his fatigue dropping from him like a cast-off garment.

The sound was nearer. Someone—and he'd be willing to bet it was Shea—was crying her eyes out.

When he came around a bend in the path, he saw her immediately. She was sitting on the ground in the shade of a birch, her head resting on her knees, her hands clasping her ankles. She was weeping as though she would never stop, her whole body shaking with emotion.

Not wanting to scare her, he said her name. Her head jerked up. He must have looked enormous standing in the shadow of the tree. She gave a cry of fear, then stammered, "S-Simon...oh, God, go away, please go away."

He dropped to his knees beside her and pulled her into his lap. Feebly she struggled against him, sobbing with an abandon that frightened him. "Tell me what's wrong," he demanded.

"Nothing. Everything. Half an hour ago I thought you were d-dead."

She fell against his chest, putting her arms around his neck in a stranglehold, and sobbed all the harder. Simon rhythmically stroked her back with one hand, ignoring the pain in his throat to whisper endearments into her ear. Finally he said, "I'm not dead. Thanks to you. Although breathing would be easier if you let go of my neck."

She looked up, her eyes still awash with tears. But she did loosen her hold. "Your face," she gasped, "that's an awful burn. Simon, you must be exhausted."

"I feel wonderful," he said forcefully. "I'm alive and I'm holding you in my arms, what more could I ask? Why are you crying, Shea?"

She glanced at her hands, which were shaking like leaves. "If my boss could see me now, he'd never let me near the controls of a helicopter again."

"While you were in the helicopter you did everything right," Simon said matter-of-factly. "You're allowed to fall apart now that it's over."

"I've never behaved like this before. It's because it was you I was rescuing. And I've lost a water bucket—that's a first, too." She shivered. "I couldn't risk landing with it. The landing was enough of a risk as it was."

"If it was a choice of me or the water bucket, I'm glad you chose me," Simon said feelingly. "You should get a medal for that landing, Shea."

"You should get one for rescuing Everett." She tried very hard to smile. "Just don't ever tell Bill Dugan how close we were to the flames."

Her fingers were still trembling. As he began rubbing them gently between his own, her face changed. "Look at your hands," she wailed, fresh tears coursing down her cheeks. "Simon, you could have died."

His nails were torn and broken from his precipitate climb up the gully. He said in a strange voice, "You care that much?"

"Of course I do, I love you." She wept. "Why else do you think I'm sitting here bawling like a baby?"

Simon's hands grew still. "Say that again."

She scrubbed at her eyes, taking several deep, heaving breaths in an effort to calm herself. "I got the message from Steve when they arrived back at the truck that you and Everett were missing," she quavered. "I thought Everett must have done something dreadful to you. I was so frightened."

"Everett came to warn me that we should leave."

"He *did*?" Blank astonishment momentarily banished her tears. "People are funny," she said. "I never——"

Scarcely listening, wondering if he had dreamed those three small words, Simon interrupted her. "Shea, did you really say you love me?"

"Well, yes, that's why I'm trying to tell you what happened. And that's why I c-can't stop crying."

In huge understatement he said, "I don't think it's an occasion for tears."

"Don't you see what it means? I didn't want to fall in love with you—and now I have." Her breath caught in a hiccup. "You just about had to die for me to realize how I felt about you. I've been so stupid."

Simon pushed a damp strand of hair back from her face and said strongly, "Sweetheart, you're going about this all the wrong way. I love you. I love you today, I'll love you tomorrow, I'll love you as long as there's breath in my body. . . and I'll love you even if you have to fight forest fires every summer until you're sixty-five. Have you got that?"

She was gazing at him wide-eyed. "I—I guess so."

"You're scared out of your wits because you're vulnerable again. I swear on my much touted honor that I'll always be there for you, Shea. Always. But I can't prove that to you now—it'll take my whole life to show you that I mean what I'm saying. There are no real answers that'll serve us once and for all."

"Trust," she whispered.

"Trust and love."

"When I brought the helicopter around and saw that the sheds had vanished, swallowed up in flames, I thought I was too late to ever tell you how I felt." Picking at a Velcro tab on his overalls, she went on in a low voice, "It was the worst moment of my life. I had the most terrible sensation of waste—as though I'd thrown away something incredibly precious."

Hope was coursing through Simon's veins. "But you don't have to feel that way any more. I'm here beside you and that's where I want to be for the rest of my life."

She looked up at him, her lashes wet, her chin raised. "I want to keep my job."

"I wouldn't have thought otherwise." He grinned at her. "Can helicopter pilots get maternity leave?"

Answering laughter glinted in her eyes. "Aren't you getting a little ahead of yourself?"

He caught her hand in his, pressing it to his lips. "Don't you see, Shea? You'll have all that you wanted. Your job, a man who loves you and whom you love, and, I hope, children."

She said quietly, "It won't always be easy."

"No, I don't suppose it will. But together we can move mountains."

"Together we can climb down pine trees," she said with a watery chuckle.

"You really do love me?" he said urgently. "You're sure?"

Her smile was suddenly radiant. "I do love you, Simon," she said.

So the fire that had almost killed him had given him an immeasurable gift. "Say it again," he ordered. "I don't think I can hear those words often enough."

She ran her fingertip along the curve of his mouth. "Didn't your mother teach you to say please?"

"Dearest Shea," he said, "darling Shea, whom I adore, please tell me you love me. Just so I'll know this is real and I haven't landed among the angels."

She shifted more comfortably in his lap, taking his dirty face in her hands. Very seriously she said, "Simon, I love you. I've loved you for a long time, but I was too scared to admit the truth."

"I love you, too." He kissed her with all the ardency of a man who only a short time ago had thought he might never see her again. Then he broke away, rubbing at a smear of soot on her cheek. "I shouldn't even be touching you, I'm filthy."

"You're alive," she said with a fervor he found irresistible, and kissed him full on the mouth.

Feeling as though he held the sun and the moon and all the stars in his arms, Simon said, "Will you marry me?"

"Yes," she said.

He threw back his head and laughed for sheer joy. "No ifs, ands or buts?"

"We've got a lifetime to work on those."

"I'll move to Nova Scotia, that's a start," he said.

"It would be easier to make love if we lived on the same side of the Atlantic," she said impishly. "Oh, Simon, I can't believe I'm so happy now and only an hour ago I thought the world had come to an end."

His mind made a sudden, crucial leap. "You knew you loved me before you landed in the clearing, right?" As she nodded, looking puzzled, he went on with growing excitement, "It must have taken every bit of your skill as a pilot to land on that rough ground and then take off before the fire reached us—don't you see what that means? It means that Shea the woman and Shea the pilot came together. They were one. Not separate."

"So I can do both," she said slowly. "I can love you and do my job. I won't ever have to push you away again the way I did that morning at Jim's apartment." Her gray eyes bemused, she said, "That's so obvious, how could I have missed it?"

"I think this forest fire has done us a huge favor."

"Kind of a drastic way for me to grow up," she said with a small smile.

He kissed her again, transferring a little more soot to her face. "The only drawback is that we won't be able to make love until the weekend," he drawled. "I don't know how I'll wait that long."

She looked at him through her lashes. "Actually Chester gave me the rest of the day off—I think he saw how shook up I was. I don't have to report in until ten tonight."

"We could steal Jim's truck and go to your cabin."

"That's a wonderful idea!"

"So you want to make love again too, do you, Shea Mallory?" He chuckled. "One look at all those black marks on your face and Chester will know what we've been up to."

"I think we should announce our engagement tonight when we get back."

He said dryly, remembering the card game, "I rather doubt it will come as a surprise."

"It did to me," Shea said.

She got up, reaching down to pull Simon to his feet. He said soberly, "Will you be all right to fly again?"

She nodded. "What about you—will you go back on ground crew?"

"If Jim'll let me—he was pretty upset." He smiled at her. "Let's tell him about the engagement when we ask for the truck."

Jim, predictably enough, was delighted, and would have given them a great deal more than the truck. Three-quarters of an hour later Simon led the way into Shea's cabin. "I'm not even going to touch you until I get cleaned up," he said. "How's that for willpower?"

She had just caught sight of the streaks of soot on her face in the mirror. "Good idea," she said.

Simon went through a lot of soap and shampoo the first few minutes; the burn on his cheek hurt horribly, and the soap stung as it found the rips in his fingers. He was letting the hot water pummel the soreness in his shoulders when Shea slipped into the cubicle with him; she was trying very hard to look as though she did this kind of thing every day.

"You've got bruises all over," she said.

"I'll survive," he replied, scarcely able to drag his eyes from her wet, lissom beauty. He took the soap, lathering the curves of her body, so well remembered, so much desired, his hands lingering on her breasts and hips. Then, overcome by his need of her, he turned off the water, wrapped her in a towel and carried her through to her bedroom. "You're a lightweight after Everett," he teased, and for the next few minutes said nothing at all, letting his body tell her of his hunger and his love.

She, too, could be impatient. But when she pulled him into her, her eyes darkening fiercely, it was she who broke the silence. "Simon, I love you," she said, and in her face was both pride and surrender.

He never wanted to tame her pride, even as he cherished her surrender. "It will take forever to show you how much I love you," he said huskily, and felt the gathering of his own surrender in the depths of her body. He moved within her as her breathing quickened, watching her control shatter and only then allowing his own to give way.

They lay together for a long time, talking, sleeping a little, touching each other in fresh delight; then Shea insisted on putting a dressing on the burn on his cheek. Afterward they cooked a rather haphazard meal, their minds not always on the menu. At nine-fifteen they wandered hand in hand along the winding path from her cabin to the driveway, under a canopy of leaves that rustled in the darkness. And Simon, deeply happy, knew he had a lifetime of walking with this woman at his side.

EPILOGUE

LATE Saturday afternoon Simon and Shea were walking up another path, the one through Minnie's garden. They had made love earlier in Shea's bed at the cabin, a love-making infinitely precious to Simon because it had been an avowal of shared emotion. In the fusion of their naked bodies had been the fusion of their souls, he thought, smiling down at Shea and lightly brushing the blue shadows under her eyes. "You look like a woman who's been well and truly loved," he said.

Her cheeks were a soft pink and her eyes shone. "I'm happier than I thought it possible to be."

The silver leaves of the poppies were hung with tiny drops of water, for it had rained for two days, a heavy downpour that had brought the forest fire under control for the first time all week. As the dampness soaked through his thin pants, Simon said very quietly, "You're my life, Shea."

"And you mine."

The trailer door opened and Minnie called, "I hear you two are getting married."

Shea chuckled. "We should have known we couldn't keep a secret from Minnie." Raising her voice, she called back, "You're invited."

"And you brought my painting," Minnie went on, eyeing the parcel under Simon's arm. "Come in, I've made two pans of butterscotch squares."

"I'll have to get the recipe," Shea said.

"It's all show, Minnie," Simon said lazily. "She's pretending she's going to be domesticated."

"In the winter I will be," Shea said indignantly. "But in the summer you'll have to visit Minnie if you want butterscotch squares."

Shea also was carrying a parcel, the larger of the two oils of Tigger. Minnie unwrapped that one first. "It's lovely," she said sincerely, blinking a little. "How well you remembered him, Simon. But I didn't expect you to do two paintings."

As she tore at the paper on the larger work, Simon watched her face. Although nothing could take away his inner certainty that the portrait was good, he very much wanted Minnie to like it, too.

The brown paper fell away and Minnie tilted the panel to the light. For a long moment she was silent. Then she said softly, "I wish my Arnold were here to see this . . . in a way he's in the painting, isn't he? Him, and Tigger, and me and my garden. All of us."

The kettle screeched on the stove. As Shea went to turn it off, Minnie said simply, "Thank you, Simon. I'll treasure it always."

A couple of hours later Shea and Simon went to Jim's for a celebratory dinner. And on Monday when Shea went back to work, Simon started work on a portrait. It was to be his wedding gift to Shea, a portrait for her eyes alone, done from the sketch that she had kept on the wall.

Shea as he had first seen her, gilded by the morning sun, naked among the water lilies.

HARLEQUIN®

PRESENTS *Plus*

When Prince Uzziah invited Beth back to his sumptuous palace, she thought he was about to sell her the Arab stallion of her dreams. But Uzziah had another deal on his mind—a race...where the winner took all....

Kelda had always clashed with her stepbrother, Angelo, but now he was interfering in her life. He claimed it was for family reasons, and he demanded Kelda enter into a new relationship with him—as his mistress!

What would you do if *you* were Beth or Kelda? Share their pleasure and their passion—watch for:

Beth and the Barbarian by Miranda Lee
Harlequin Presents Plus #1711

and

Angel of Darkness by Lynne Graham
Harlequin Presents Plus #1712

Harlequin Presents Plus
The best has just gotten better!

Available in January wherever Harlequin books are sold.

MILLION DOLLAR SWEEPSTAKES (III)

No purchase necessary. To enter, follow the directions published. Method of entry may vary. For eligibility, entries must be received no later than March 31, 1996. No liability is assumed for printing errors, lost, late or misdirected entries. Odds of winning are determined by the number of eligible entries distributed and received. Prizewinners will be determined no later than June 30, 1996.

Sweepstakes open to residents of the U.S. (except Puerto Rico), Canada, Europe and Taiwan who are 18 years of age or older. All applicable laws and regulations apply. Sweepstakes offer void wherever prohibited by law. Values of all prizes are in U.S. currency. This sweepstakes is presented by Torstar Corp., its subsidiaries and affiliates, in conjunction with book, merchandise and/or product offerings. For a copy of the Official Rules send a self-addressed, stamped envelope (WA residents need not affix return postage) to: MILLION DOLLAR SWEEPSTAKES (III) Rules, P.O. Box 4573, Blair, NE 68009, USA.

EXTRA BONUS PRIZE DRAWING

No purchase necessary. The Extra Bonus Prize will be awarded in a random drawing to be conducted no later than 5/30/96 from among all entries received. To qualify, entries must be received by 3/31/96 and comply with published directions. Drawing open to residents of the U.S. (except Puerto Rico), Canada, Europe and Taiwan who are 18 years of age or older. All applicable laws and regulations apply; offer void wherever prohibited by law. Odds of winning are dependent upon number of eligibile entries received. Prize is valued in U.S. currency. The offer is presented by Torstar Corp., its subsidiaries and affiliates in conjunction with book, merchandise and/or product offering. For a copy of the Official Rules governing this sweepstakes, send a self-addressed, stamped envelope (WA residents need not affix return postage) to: Extra Bonus Prize Drawing Rules, P.O. Box 4590, Blair, NE 68009, USA.

SWP-H1294

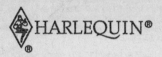 **HARLEQUIN**®

 *Weddings, Inc.*

The proprietors of Weddings, Inc. hope you
have enjoyed visiting Eternity, Massachusetts.
And if you missed any of the exciting Weddings,
Inc. titles, here is your opportunity to complete
your collection:

Harlequin Superromance	#598	*Wedding Invitation* by Marisa Carroll	$3.50 U.S. $3.99 CAN.	☐ ☐
Harlequin Romance	#3319	*Expectations* by Shannon Waverly	$2.99 U.S. $3.50 CAN.	☐ ☐
Harlequin Temptation	#502	*Wedding Song* by Vicki Lewis Thompson	$2.99 U.S. $3.50 CAN.	☐ ☐
Harlequin American Romance	#549	*The Wedding Gamble* by Muriel Jensen	$3.50 U.S. $3.99 CAN.	☐ ☐
Harlequin Presents	#1692	*The Vengeful Groom* by Sara Wood	$2.99 U.S. $3.50 CAN.	☐ ☐
Harlequin Intrigue	#298	*Edge of Eternity* by Jasmine Cresswell	$2.99 U.S. $3.50 CAN.	☐ ☐
Harlequin Historical	#248	*Vows* by Margaret Moore	$3.99 U.S. $4.50 CAN.	☐ ☐

HARLEQUIN BOOKS...
NOT THE SAME OLD STORY

TOTAL AMOUNT	$
POSTAGE & HANDLING ($1.00 for one book, 50¢ for each additional)	$
APPLICABLE TAXES*	$
TOTAL PAYABLE (check or money order—please do not send cash)	$

To order, complete this form and send it, along with a check or money order for the
total above, payable to Harlequin Books, to: **In the U.S.:** 3010 Walden Avenue,
P.O. Box 9047, Buffalo, NY 14269-9047; **In Canada:** P.O. Box 613, Fort Erie, Ontario,
L2A 5X3.

Name: _____

Address: _____ City: _____

State/Prov.: _____ Zip/Postal Code: _____

*New York residents remit applicable sales taxes.
Canadian residents remit applicable GST and provincial taxes.

WED-F